MW01093484

THE 14TH DENIAL:
A CIVIL RIGHTS MEMOIR

i

2019

THIS BOOK IS FOR FELLOW
PATRIOT JAY SEKULOW,
   GOOD HEALTH, GOOD LUCK
AND GOD BLESS YOU.

DET SGT. CANNER LEE CODY

Additional copies of the 14th Denial may be ordered from the publisher or from your favorite online or neighborhood bookstore.

THE 14TH DENIAL: A CIVIL RIGHTS MEMOIR

Detective Sergeant Cannie Lee Cody

with Professor Rickey E. Pittman

To Lieutenant Ray O. Headen

One of the finest law enforcement officers I have ever known

and to Johnnie Mae Chappell (1929-1964)

It is your story I wanted to tell . . . .

Table of Contents

PREFACE

Whistle-blowers are not your ordinary citizens. In fact, even though it is the right thing to do, they have got to be a little crazy, because a lot of bad things happen to them afterward.
—*Peter Maas, New York Times, 29 Jan. 1986.*

Cannie Lee Cody, Jr. worked in Jacksonville, Florida, with the Duval County Sheriff's Office for seven years, reaching the rank of Detective Sergeant. In 1964, in the midst of the volatile times surrounding the Civil Rights Movement, Sergeants Cannie Lee Cody, Jr. and Donald R. Coleman, Sr., solved one of our nation's worst hate crimes and paid for it with their careers.

In the years since, Cody has collected and catalogued a mountain of documents providing irrefutable evidence that exposes blatant racism prevalent in high places—in both federal and state offices—and he has created a horrifying tale of cover-ups and corruption resulting in flagrant violations of the 14th Amendment and a disregard for the Civil Rights guaranteed citizens under our nation's Constitution for equal protection under the law's.

As told in part on *Oprah, the History Channel, Court TV*, and *Dateline*, this is the tragic story of the premeditated murder of Johnnie Mae Chappell, a thirty-five-year-old law-abiding black mother of ten and after her murder, the decade's long criminal obstruction of justice. It is a story of racism and public corruption at its ugliest.

In addition to the racism, Cody's expose also reveals the persecution of the Duval County detectives who solved the Chappell homicide and their attempts to bring the guilty to justice. Cody details the massive conspiracy on the part of law enforcement and government officials and prosecutors orchestrated by both state and federal officials—including even members of the FBI, who were determined to cover up for those responsible for the criminal obstruction of justice in Johnnie Mae Chappell's murder—especially Duval County's Sheriff Dale Carson, a former FBI agent; Duval County Chief of Detectives James Calvin Patrick, Sr., a graduate of the FBI Academy. The amount and degree of governmental corruption, obstruction of justice, and Civil Rights violations that Detective Sergeants Cody and Coleman and other dedicated detectives discovered is voluminous.

For years, Sergeants Cody and Coleman sought vindication and exposure of the guilty officials. Their offers to supply documentation, witnesses and evidence were refused and/or ignored by every official of every state and federal office warranted by oath of office to act upon this evidence. At last, with the publication of this book, Sergeant Cody has his chance to tell his story. *The 14th Denial* is a documented account that Sergeant Cody hopes every American has a chance to read.

The 14ᵗʰ Amendment

Passed by Congress June 13, 1866. Ratified July 9, 1868.

Section 1.

All persons born or naturalized in the United States, and subject to the jurisdiction thereof, are citizens of the United States and of the State wherein they reside. No State shall make or enforce any law which shall abridge the privileges or immunities of citizens of the United States; nor shall any State deprive any person of life, liberty, or property, without due process of law; nor deny to any person within its jurisdiction the equal protection of the laws.

Chapter One:

Just Another Night in Jacksonville

August 7, 1964

I remember standing here / right on this very same site / I was dying, but for you /it was just another night—Cat Stevens, "Just Another Night"

Even in those days, there was no shortage of work for detectives. This night, Detective Sergeants C. Lee Cody and Donald R. Coleman were working their contacts on the four to midnight shift in northwest Duval County, a predominantly black area. They knew every moonshine bumper joint—so-called because the moonshine there was sold in twenty-five cent bumper shots—and they knew every white roadhouse in Northeast Florida as well. They knew of the "skin" games and the cathouses operating in Jacksonville and throughout Duval County. The most infamous bordello that ever operated in Duval County was named the Green Lantern, which ironically was located on Moncrief Road, not too far from the location where Johnnie Mae Chappell would be murdered. In the fifties urban sprawl resulted in the Green Lantern's closure, and most of the prostitutes who worked there moved into downtown Jacksonville hotels and dilapidated tourist courts on Highway 17, such as the Fire Chief and Howell's Cabins.

In short, the two knew the denizens and activities of the city of Jacksonville and Duval County's dark underbellies well, and from their informants and contacts at these rough places of business, they regularly garnered the information they needed to make arrests or hopefully stop a criminal before he could commit a planned crime. The regulation of these places in the unincorporated areas of Duval County came under the auspices of the Vice Squad Division of the Sheriff's Office. The Vice division, headed by Lieutenant Jim Hamlin whose office was immediately adjacent to Sheriff Carson's office. Hamlin would regularly communicate to Duval County Sheriff's Office officers the "official" policy regulating each club. That clearly stated policy was often, "It's okay to make an appearance, but hands off," indicating the club was under the sheriff's "protection." It was clearly understood that the Vice Squad Division would regulate the clubs and take care of any problems or legal code violations and collect whatever gratuities were due the Sheriff's Office for favors or protection extended.

Some nights Cody and Coleman would drop in on dives with unforgettable names like the Alligator Lady, the Red Rooster, the Black Shack, and Bo Weaver's Pine Inn. There were contacts there like Yay-Yay, a Cuban who ran the Havana Night Club, which was located on Avenue B. They would talk with informants like Algie, a huge black man who ran the Silver Star. The clientele of these places were black generally, with crowds that ran from the civil and gentile to rough and dangerous. Algie was big, bold, and blustering, but one night he confronted a belligerent customer who capped him in the chest with three bullets. Duval County lost a valuable contact that night.

Not all of the clubs were dives. Some establishments were high-class clubs, like the famous *2 Spot*, where famous and fabulous black performers like B. B. King,

Dinah Washington, Sam Cooke, James Brown, Lionel Hampton, Ruth Brown, Charlie Singleton, and Jackie Wilson performed to segregated black and white audiences. White patrons would be escorted to the balcony—an ironic twist to the days when black visitors were consigned to the balconies of theatres and churches.

This night the detectives chose to drop in on Yay-Yay's Havana nightclub. Once inside, as usual a big and exuberant black woman named Bolita who managed the Havana met them. Bolita knew the detectives well enough to know they were not racists and though she was well aware of her black "status," she felt comfortable enough to kid them now and then. She always greeted the detectives warmly saying, "Hello, Sergeant Cody and Sergeant Coleman—the two most handsome policemen I know. One of these days, Bolita is gonna change your luck!"

"In my dreams," Sergeant Cody said.

Bolita was named after the illegal gambling lottery that had originated in Cuba. The odds were usually 60-70 to one, and tickets for this extremely profitable enterprise were sold everywhere in Florida in low-end bars, pool halls, and stores—stores that often seemed to be run by people of Middle Eastern extraction. The winning numbers came to Florida from Cuba. The lottery business in Florida was supposedly controlled by Mafioso boss, Santo Trafficante, Jr., in Tampa, an operation very similar to that ran in New York City by Dutch Shultz. Trafficante also operated casinos in Cuba and maintained a private residence in Havana. This was during the reign of the dictator, Batista. Castro's revolution was underway, but Castro's forces at that time, though impressive, were still the underdog in that conflict. To hedge his bets, Trafficante contributed monies to both Castro and Batista. However, once Castro gained power, the dictator confiscated Trafficante's casinos, his home, and his bank accounts and jailed him. Eventually, Trafficante was released from confinement and returned to Florida to resume his business.

Persistent rumors indicated that men like Trafficante, Jimmy Hoffa and Carlos Marcello, the Mafia chief in New Orleans, were somehow involved in or connected to John F. Kennedy's and Lee Harvey Oswald's assassination. Shortly after Kennedy's assassination, Frank Regan, the lawyer who had represented these mob figures, publicly stated in a TV documentary of his life that he was directed by Carolos Marcello to deliver a message to Teamster leader Jimmy Hoffa. The message was simply: "You owe me, and you owe me big."

In the days when Robert Kennedy was Attorney General and went after organized crime, it was widely believed this unholy trinity—Tropicante, Marcello, and Hoffa—allied themselves and thought about killing Robert Kennedy. However, it appears they instead decided to go after the head of the snake. When John F. Kennedy was assassinated, Robert Kennedy resigned from the office of Attorney General. A few months later, he was then not a problem to organized crime. However, when Robert Kennedy regained national prominence and became the frontrunner for the office of President, the rumors again persisted that the unholy trinity acted again, and he too was assassinated.

When the detectives told Bolita they had come to see Yay-Yay, she led them to the manager's office in the back of the nightclub.

It was just one of those hot, humid, quiet Jacksonville nights that seemed to drag on forever, a night when the thugs were still and there were no calls, no murders, and no robberies to investigate. The detectives thought it would just be just another night when they would make the town feel their presence and return to the office

4

for the routine end-of-day paperwork, then to their wives and homes.

From the Havana, which the locals pronounced as "Hay-banna," Cody and Coleman went east to an all night drive-in burger joint across town on Lem Turner Road frequented by whites only and called the Freezette. Across from the Freezette was a Syrian grocery whose owner often sold the detectives discounted steaks that the Freezette's owner, Bob Perry, would cook for the detectives while they passed a hunk of their evening eating and easing information out of Perry, who was another of their informants. While Perry cooked their steak and Cody and Coleman compared notes and thoughts, Cody noticed a white male, Wayne Chessman, a twenty-one-year-old tough whom Cody knew, sitting at a table near them. Cody had only been a detective for six months, and prior to that had known and ticketed the man during his five years as a uniformed Duval County Patrol Officer.

Sergeant Cody nodded to him. When Chessman finished eating, he rose and approached the detectives.

"Officer Cody, I just want to let you know that I'm going to straighten my life out," Chessman told him. "My mother has married a wealthy man who works for the Airlines in South Florida. He's going to get me a job, and I'm going back to school. If I can ever help you guys, call me." Then he left the Freezette.

Donald Coleman had been a detective for several years, but did not know Chessman and asked Cody, "What the hell was that about? How do you know this man?"

Cody told him how he knew the young man from the days when he was a uniformed Duval County Patrol Officer, but said he had no idea why Chessman had said what he said.

A few days later, the detectives had another slow evening and once again ended up at the Freezette. Just as they were seated, a car drove up and parked. Chessman was in the car, and this time he was with a friend, Elmer Kato. Kato drove a souped-up dark blue Plymouth with loud mufflers. Cody knew the car and the driver well. The car was notorious for being one of the fastest cars on the road, and Kato notorious for being a hot rod drag racer.

Chessman spotted the detectives through the front glass windows, and he left Kato in the car, entered the restaurant, approached the detectives, and again exclaimed to Sergeants Cody and Coleman, "I just wanted to remind you again, that if I can ever help you officers, let me know." Then, once again, he departed abruptly and returned to Kato's car, its glass-pack mufflers vibrating the windows as it left the parking lot.

Sergeants Cody and Coleman recognized guilt when they saw it. Chessman was agitated. He seemed to have a sense of urgency, like he wanted to talk about something. Cody eyed Kato through the window. "Donald, Chessman has something serious on his mind." Sergeant Cody pulled a notebook from his inside suit coat pocket and checked it. Cody liked to stay on top of what was going on in the county, particularly homicides, so he would daily record in his notebook any information that he thought was interesting or germane to current criminal activity that might help him and Coleman with their ongoing and future investigations. To garner information, he had an established habit to be at the office early every morning so he could check the daily-submitted investigative reports. This habit proved to be an effective one, for in 1964; the pair of detectives alone had solved twenty-three armed robberies by arrest and conviction, as well as a multitude of other criminal offenses. This figure was more than the combined total of the other nine detective teams in the Sheriff's Detective Division.

Earlier on March 24, 1964, Sergeant Cody had read the reports generated at the scene on the night of Ms. Chappell's death. The original investigative reports contained only the victim's name, the type and date of the offense, the names of the two reported witnesses and their description of the vehicle that the gunshot had come from. According to the on-site report, the only thing the witnesses had said with certainty about the car was that it was a dark vehicle and had left the scene at a very high rate of speed, proceeding on U. S. Highway 1 North.

"That dark car of Kato's matches the general description of the car used in the Chappell homicide on U.S. Highway 1 North on the night of the inner city race riots in March," Sergeant Cody said. "I bet you both Chessman and Kato were involved in that homicide one way or another."

North Duval County, where these men were reared, was a hotbed of activity for the Ku Klux Klan, so it would not be surprising for them to have fallen into something like this. Men in this area of Duval County were subjected to racism all their life and it is unrealistic to think that they were not influenced by their environment and capable of committing such a crime.

When Chessman first approached them, the detectives had thought it was going to be just another night on the four-to-twelve shift. It wasn't.

Chapter Two:

The Murder of
Johnny Mae Chappell

Jacksonville, Florida 1964

I have looked down the saddest city lane.
I have passed by the watchman on his beat
And dropped my eyes, unwilling to explain.
I have stood still and stopped the sound of feet
When far away an interrupted cry
Came over houses from another street . . .
--"Acquainted with the Night"
by Robert Frost

The city where Johnnie Mae Chappell was murdered, Jacksonville, Florida, has had a rich, but troubled history. The city actually had begun with Fort Caroline, established by the French in 1564. Fort Caroline was obliterated and its Protestant occupants massacred by Spanish soldiers from nearby Saint Augustine a year after Fort Caroline was built. Centered on the banks of the St. John's River, Spain temporarily ceded the settlement to the British in 1763 and the town of "Cowford" was born, so called because the river was so narrow and shallow there that this was where settlers forded their cattle. Changing hands again in 1821 when Florida Territory was acquired from Spain and became part of the United States. Cowford was renamed Jacksonville, in honor of Andrew Jackson, the first governor of Florida and the seventh President of the United States.

It is a city where one has always been able to encounter the violent, the strange or macabre. For example, it was in Jacksonville, Florida where Dr. Frederick Wheedon, the best white friend and attending physician of the Seminole warrior Osceola, had a practice and pharmacy. After Osceola's death from a fever, the good doctor decapitated the chief's head, embalmed it in a jar of alcohol and displayed it in his storefront window. He was said to have also used the head to frighten his teenage sons at night when they misbehaved.

Ravaged by fire and fever throughout its history, Jacksonville, sometimes known as "Jax," is the largest city in the U.S. in land area. At one time or another, the city has been a center for the film industry and a resort and a playground for the wealthy. And more significantly, to this story, Duval County had long been a hotbed for the Klan. Jacksonville is a city where the bloody veins of racial prejudice and suspicion have run deep and sometimes violent. Detective Cody recalls a story related to him by his grandmother, Emma Dukes, how as a young woman she had observed a black man being dragged down Bay Street in Jacksonville while chained to a car. Cody never forgot that story. The story of Johnnie Mae Chappell must be understood in the racially charged context of Duval County.

Riots had broken out in 1960 in the incorporated portion of Duval County, which contained the city of Jacksonville. One incident that drew national attention in the news media was labeled as *Axe Handle Saturday*. The city police had been overwhelmed by the mob violence and had called for the help of the Sheriff's Office. Cody had been there with the Duval County Road Patrol. Cody says the incident was violent and bloody and precipitated by Klan members who with deodorant sprayed the heads of young black males and females asking to be served at the lunch counter at Woolworth's. Violence erupted and spilled from the store into the streets.

Another riot occurred on March 23 of 1964. On that night, Mrs. Chappell was shot. Black citizens of Jacksonville, weary of the continual hardships of discrimination, had organized protests downtown. According to a USA Today article, when fires were set and some demonstrations escalated into street fights, Mayor and Police Commissioner Haydon Burns, committed to segregation, and equally determined to end the demonstrations, deputized 496 firemen, to assist law enforcement control the riots. However, Detective Cody points out that the mayor could not legally deputize anyone, as the mayor did not have that authority. Only Duval County Sheriff Dale Carson had the authority to deputize any citizen. What Burns had actually done was to appoint firemen as special police officers for the City of Jacksonville with the powers of arrest only in the city limits.

Johnnie Mae Chappell, a mother of ten, lived in the northwest quadrant of Duval County, which then was occupied by 95% black families and businesses. Mrs. Chappell, a domestic worker, and her husband Willie were known to be hardworking and law-abiding citizens, but their combined salaries did not make much of a living. The going rate for a domestic worker, doing what was known as "days work," was three dollars a day. Mrs. Chappell's husband worked two jobs as a cement finisher in the day and gas station attendant at night, but still, in spite of all their efforts, what they brought in was barely enough to provide for their ten children.

Johnnie Mae had returned home by bus from her typical grueling day at her job, about 15 miles away, and then walked to the Banner Store near the bus stop. After preparing supper and tending to the needs of her family, she realized she had lost her wallet. In those days, there were no plastic sacks, and the paper sack she carried had split because of the moisture from the ice cream she had purchased. A mother of ten, a woman who worked for the wealthy and whose main concern was taking care of her family, she had no interest and likely little knowledge of the riots exploding downtown.

Thinking of her family and their needs, Johnnie Mae borrowed a flashlight and enlisted the help of neighbors, Albert Smith and Tildia Sanders, to look for the missing wallet. She retraced her steps all the way to the market on New King's Road, about a quarter of a mile in distance. According to the witnesses, who were briefly interviewed by the detectives dispatched to the scene, a dark sedan had slowed on U.S. 1 just north of Moncrief Road, a shot was fired from the vehicle's open front window, and Johnnie Mae Chappell tumbled to the ground. After a moment and with great effort, Johnnie Mae rose and staggered across U.S. 1. She then fell to the ground in front of the Banner Food Market where she had only a short time earlier purchased ice cream for her ten children.

One of those with her hurriedly called for the police and an ambulance. The Duval County Road Patrol officers were as usual the first on the scene. Officer William Plaster stated that he cradled her in his arms, telling her not to worry, that an ambulance was on the way.

"Oh, no, Mr. Policeman," Johnnie Mae said. "I'm going to die."

Officer Plaster did his best to comfort her. He stayed with her until the ambulance arrived. He later said in a History Channel interview that he was touched by the experience and said that he would never forget that evening.

In those days, black citizens were only transported in designated "colored" ambulances and only taken to designated "colored" hospitals—even if they were dying.

Johnnie Mae was taken to the Duval County Medical Center (County Hospital). The emergency room there was understaffed and usually overwhelmed with trauma cases, such as knife and gunshot wound victims, and it was widely believed that if you were sent there, your chances of survival were not very good. As the ambulances used were actually hearses belonging to funeral homes and the drivers were funeral home employees or morticians, many injured black Americans would refuse to ride in them. They feared what they had heard from others in their community—that they would be smothered—perhaps by a greedy funeral director—and not reach the hospital alive. As autopsies were usually not performed on blacks in those days—with the exception of reported homicides—no one would know what the real cause of death was and the insured funeral home vehicle could just take the body directly from the hospital to the funeral home. Sergeant Cody recalls once instance when he was a rookie-uniformed officer, when a black man who was badly injured refused to go into the ambulance (the funeral home hearse). "I don't want to go with them! I don't want to go with them!" the man said. Sergeant Cody had to physically assist the hearse driver to get the injured man onto the gurney and into the "ambulance." The man was still protesting as the vehicle drove away. At the time, it didn't make sense to Sergeant Cody. However, once he heard the ambulance stories several times from other senior officers, he understood the man's reluctance. Later he would take it upon himself to check the death certificate of any black citizen he assisted who was transported by the funeral home hearse to make sure that the injured were transported directly to the hospital and not to the funeral home.

Mrs. Chappell died en route to the hospital. She was then taken to the morgue. Shelton Chappell was only months old at the time of his mother's murder. The only photo that Shelton possesses of his mother—and indeed, the only photograph of Johnnie Mae that exists—is of her lying on that cold morgue slab. This photo was originally published by *Jet Magazine*, and was subsequently published in the *Miami Herald* and *La Times*, on *Dateline*, and on a Civil Rights Martin Luther King special shown on *Oprah*, January 2008. Of the picture, Shelton says, "Just look at that picture. It says it all."

Chapter Three:
Tush Hogs: The Men
Who Commit Murder

Tush Hog –According to Cormac McCarthy in Suttree,
a "tush hog" is a bullying, redneck white
trash boy or man.

Detectives Cody and Coleman knew all of Duval County well. They also knew the ilk of those who lived in their assigned district—both the criminals and the law-abiding citizens. The county was and is huge, and the deputies had arrest powers in the entire county, including the City of Jacksonville. The boys and young men of this area often had a rawness and rough edge to them. They were hot rodders, bar fighters, petty thieves and generally had a knack for staying in trouble. The detectives tagged these boys as "Tush Hogs." And just like the wild hogs hunted in Florida woods that they were named after, they were rough and tough, volatile, unpredictable and could be dangerous at times.

The crime the tush hogs in this story committed is clearly delineated in their sworn, court-reported confessions and transcribed on August 11-12 1964. The confessions reveal that on that night, J.W. Rich, James Alex Davis, Elmer Kato, and Wayne Chessman met at the Freezette Drive-In Restaurant around 7:00 p.m. They left and drove downtown into the teeth of the ongoing race riots. Then, after satisfying that curiosity, they drank beer and continued to cruise the riot area in Kato's dark blue 1963 Plymouth, one with deep, loud, rumbling pipes.

As they drove, they listened to the radio, probably WJAX, spouting news of the race riots and of numerous attacks taking place downtown on citizens, newsmen, and vehicles. The reports on the radio fueled their anger and their fear. Someone in the car said, "Let's go get a nigger." Chessman and Kato swore in their certified court-reported confessions that the shooter, J.W. Rich made that statement. Rich, in his confession, denied saying it, admitting only that "Somebody said it." However, as Cody points out, it doesn't matter who said it. By continuing after it was said, all four were now complicit in the crime. The spoken words were like the words of a wizard, powerful and goading the boys on in that night's dark path. The conspirators then decided to drive to the northwest quadrant of Duval County, knowing well that this was a predominantly black area of town.

Eventually, they drove by three black pedestrians walking south along New Kings Road. Kato slowed the vehicle, and then Rich picked up Chessman's .22 pistol from the seat and fired out the front passenger side window. In Rich's own words, he then "saw one of the niggers go down" as they sped off. Later, Rich attested he was only acting the fool and the gun went off by accident. However, according to Detective Sergeants Cody and Coleman, the compiled investigative facts absolutely deny Rich's contention.

The four lived with the secret of Johnnie Mae's murder from March 23 until August 11, 1964, when Detectives Cody and Coleman uncovered the involvement of the tush hogs in the murder of Johnnie Mae Chappell.

*   *   *

Good detectives develop an intuitive intelligence and can often read people and the subtleties of the human mind well, especially the minds of criminals. When the detectives arrived at the office for their 4:00 p.m. - 12:00 a.m. shift on the day after Chessman approached them, with his suspicions aroused, Detective Cody made the suggestion to his senior partner Coleman that they obtain a Bible from the library in the Detective Division. He found the Bible, then took a red pen and underlined the sixth commandment of the Ten, "Thou shalt not kill."

Coleman studied Cody marking the Bible and asked, "What on earth are you thinking?"

"I'm thinking we should pick up Chessman and bring him in for questioning if he's willing. We'll put this Bible in front of him and see if it shakes anything loose."

Since Chessman had talked of changing his life and doing what's right, this idea made sense to Coleman. He said he thought it just might work.

Sergeant Cody said, "Let's do it."

Chapter Four:

Solving the Crime

My fault is past.
But, O, what form of prayer / Can serve my turn?
'Forgive me my foul murder'?

—Hamlet

Detectives Cody and Coleman went by Chessman's house at dusk. They observed Chessman lying on a sofa and they could see the light of the television shining on his socked feet. They knocked and Cody said through the screen door, "Wayne, its Sergeant Cody and Sergeant Coleman. How about coming to the door and talking to us for a minute."

Chessman complied and Cody continued. "Wayne, you've offered to help us a couple of times recently. Would you mind accompanying us to the sheriff's office? We think there is something you can help us with."

"Sure," Chessman said. "Let me get my shoes on."

At the Sheriff's Office, the sergeants Cody and Coleman escorted Chessman to the interrogation room, which like all interrogation rooms, was sparsely furnished, having only a steel table and four chairs. Sergeant Cody retrieved the departmental Bible from the drawer of the interrogation room table where he had previously placed it, opened it to the Ten Commandments and slid it across the table. "Read what is underlined in red, Wayne."

Chessman's eyes were of course drawn to the red underlined Sixth Commandment, which says, "Thou shalt not kill."

"Do you have any comments?" Cody asked.

He looked up with a startled face. "Oh, my God. I didn't shoot her, Sarge. I was just in the car."

"You didn't shoot who?" Cody asked.

"That old nigger woman on U.S. 1 during the race riots last March."

"Well, if you didn't shoot her, then who did?"

"J.W. Rich shot her. We were all in Elmer Kato's car."

"Who else was in the car?"

"Elmer was driving, J.W. was in the front seat, and Eugene Davis was in the back seat with me."

"Whose gun was it?"

Chessman said, "It was mine."

"Describe it for me, Wayne," Cody said.

"It's an H & R .22 caliber target pistol. It was blue steel with dark wood handles, and I brought it to the party."

"Would you mind submitting a sworn confession about what you've just told us?"

"Sure. I'd be more than glad to."

After Chessman's confession, it should have been a relatively easy process to wrap the case up. In those days, when the detectives made an arrest connected to a previous case to which they had not been assigned for follow-up, they would go to the records division and pull the case file. This step began with pulling from the Alpha file the 5x7-index card filled out on every case. The 5x7-index card

20

contained the victim's name, address, race, the crime, and the *assigned case number*, which would then lead them to the numerically catalogued case file. From the case file, it could be learned the identity of the detective team originally assigned to follow up the case for investigation.

The case was only a few months old, and considering the racially charged atmosphere in Jacksonville as well as across the nation, the detectives surely would have heard if there had been any developments surrounding the Chappell homicide. The detectives' obligation then would have been to identity and notify the detectives originally assigned to the case in last March for follow-up investigation. Sergeants Cody and Coleman would then communicate the recent developments, request their presence at the Sheriff's Office, brief them on the events that had resulted in their involvement, and then upon arrival of the assigned follow-up detectives, they would turn the case over to them for further investigation and prosecution. Cody and Coleman would then be free to return to their four to midnight assigned shift. It should have taken just a short or at least a reasonable amount of time to complete this procedure, and if this procedure had taken place, Cody and Coleman would have had no further involvement in the case until called upon to testify, unless the case detectives asked for their assistance.

Yet, complications began immediately. They went to the 5 x 7-index card file to find the case number. The index card for Johnnie Mae Chappell's murder could not be found. This presented a serious problem for the detectives, one they had never experienced before. It would not be uncommon for a case file not to be present. It could be in the hands of the Sheriff, Chief, assigned case detectives or other Sheriff's Office investigative personnel. The 5 x 7 card would NEVER be missing. The index cards were points of reference for every case and were not to be removed for any reason, for they contained the most important reference information—the case file number. The case files contained the on-site investigative reports as well as all pertinent follow-up investigative results.

They next went to search an additional source of information, the Daily Bulletin, which hung on the wall in the Detective Division. The Daily Bulletin contained each and every offense reported, each stamped with a sequential case number that had been affixed by the duty lieutenant on the date of receipt. These case numbers were affixed by a mechanical stamping device. The Detective Division clerk, John Keane, would then transcribe these case numbers and a brief case description. The information would be posted then on legal-size paper and fastened onto a large ringed clipboard. The Daily Bulletin would be readily available at all times for scrutiny. Most Sheriff's Office reports in 1964 in their original form were written cursively, but in this case, as was true of all homicide cases, it would have been retyped by a secretary, primarily because the medical examiner demanded/required typed reports for all homicides.

The detectives could find no entry in the Daily Bulletin related to Johnnie Mae Chappell's homicide on March 23, 1964—nothing. The detectives began feeling an unsettling consternation. They had a confessed conspirator in the Chappell homicide who had identified the shooter and two other conspirators, but they had no case number or no case file.

"Maybe the file's in the chief's office," Coleman said.

"Let's take a look," Cody replied. The detectives who had the evening shift each had a key to the chief's office with permission to access the Chief of Detective's office because that is where the radios, car keys and other pieces of equipment were kept. Since they knew that Chief J.C. Patrick also occasionally examined case files himself, and had a habit of piling them along his office wall, it seemed like a logical place to look. Johnnie Mae Chappell's case file would have everything they needed to tie up their loose ends. It would have contained the original reports, cursively written onsite, the retyped reports to medical examiner's office, and the names and supplementary reports of the detective teams that had conducted the follow-up investigation. However, though there were some files stacked around the office, Chappell's case could not be found.

"We've got to get some help," Cody told Coleman. Cody contacted the dispatcher, saying, "Get us some help. We'll need two court reporters. And some other detectives. I don't care who. We have other suspects we have to pick up quickly. You might as well call Chief Patrick. If he's not on the radio or at home, call M&M Liquor on Beach Boulevard, [his daily watering hole] and ask him to come to the office."

Though help was on the way, the detectives still felt they needed to find the vital case number. "What do we do now, Coleman?" Cody said.

We'll just have to wing it, I guess," Coleman said as he plopped himself into the chief's chair. As he sat, the chair rolled a bit and he noticed the corner of a white paper protruding from under the chair's mat. Coleman looked at it a moment and then said, "I wonder what this might be?"

Cody said, "I don't know. Let's take a look."

Coleman lifted the mat and the detectives observed what appeared to be thirty to forty individual pages of various reports. Unbelievably, the exposed paper that Coleman had first seen was the typed County Road Patrol Addendum to the Chappell homicide. This addendum was a worksheet that identified the first officers on the scene and indicated what they had observed and found. This addendum is one that the uniformed officers on the scene were obligated to submit. In this case, the County Patrol Officer who filed the report was William Plaster, and the case number they needed was stamped on the top right corner. This would provide them with enough information to locate and identify the file and hopefully solve their problems and enable them to contact the assigned case detectives.

At least, they thought so.

However, this fortunate discovery also caused some other worries. Their suspicions were now raised. There was obviously something amiss here, and it was obvious to both detectives that Chief Patrick had to be directly involved. But how? The Chief of Detectives doesn't just separate a single document from its file and hide it under his office chair mat for any legitimate official reason. The detectives wanted to sift through the remaining stack of papers hoping to locate the rest of the missing Chappell homicide file, but were unable to continue searching because they knew that Chief Patrick would arrive soon, and past experiences suggested that he would likely be highly intoxicated. The detectives did not know what to expect if Chief Patrick were to see the addendum on their desk, but as Patrick possessed a volatile temper, they didn't think he would be happy about their "accidental" discovery.

From the Chief of Detective's office, they went to the Records Division again, hoping to retrieve the file now that they had the needed case number. The case file wasn't there. This was the point when the detectives realized that there was strong evidence that obstruction of justice in a capital Civil Rights hate crime homicide had occurred.

The evidence they had uncovered already could not by any stretch of the imagination be attributed to sloppy police work or misfiling. The detectives suspected that Chief Patrick was the obstruction architect. At this juncture, detectives Cody and Coleman decided to keep quiet and at an appropriate time present their evidence to Sheriff Carson. It was too late now for them to go back to the chief's office and look further, though they were certain that if they had been given more time, they would have found the full Chappell homicide case file under the mat as well as the missing 5x7 index card. There was no justifiable legal reason for Chief Patrick to have any part of the case file hidden under his chair mat, and it didn't make sense to think that he would have only shuffled aside the uniformed officers' addendum.

When Chief of Detectives J.C. Patrick arrived, he was indeed highly intoxicated, as he usually was this time of the evening. Sergeants Cody and Coleman, having been subjected to this embarrassment before, were not surprised. Every afternoon, on his way home, Patrick would stop at M. & M. Liquors on Beach Boulevard and load up on free vodka. Chief Patrick would even often show up at a crime scene highly intoxicated. Chief Patrick didn't have much to say, and he did not seem to notice the addendum—now in plain sight—that the detectives had retrieved from under his chair mat. Detectives were dispatched to take into custody the other suspects named by Wayne Chessman. After they were taken into custody, certified, court reported confessions were obtained from Wayne Chessman, J.W. Rich and Elmer Kato. James Davis had joined the Army and recently left the area, so he could not be taken into custody.

As it was now apparent that no detectives had ever been assigned to conduct a follow-up investigation of the Chappell homicide, Sergeants Cody and Coleman became legally obligated to complete the investigative matters made known to them on the night of August 11 and morning of August 12, thereby becoming by virtue of circumstance the Chappell homicide case detectives.

The next day the detectives continued their search for information on the Chappell homicide and the missing case files. They knew they had to be careful because after all, they were investigating what appeared to be criminal obstruction of justice on the part of their Chief of Detectives and God only knows whom else. They were also acutely aware that Chief Patrick had many eyes. Knowing the City Police Department was regularly furnished a copy of the Sheriff's Office's Daily Bulletin, and to escape the eyes of Patrick's spies, they thought they would start looking there. The detectives frequently had business at that location, so they knew their presence would attract no attention.

After a thorough search, the officers finally found the case number that matched the number on Officer Plaster's addendum—number 4498. However, it had been a case file assigned to a lawnmower theft. To make sure, they checked the Daily Bulletin entries for the entire month of March. There was nothing related to the Johnnie Mae Chappell homicide, nor any insertion that bore her name. Having previously been unable to find a case file or the 5x7 index card relating to the Johnnie Mae Chappell homicide in the Duval County Sheriff's Office records, it was obvious at this point to the detectives that there had been a deliberate attempt to obliterate any Sheriff's Office records pertaining to the Johnnie Mae Chappell homicide.

Still, the detectives pressed on. They were determined to bring this unusual set of circumstances to an understandable conclusion, and if possible, expose the obstructer or obstructers. They had all but one of the confessed Chappell assailants in custody. Now, they needed the murder weapon, which Chessman had described as a .22 H & R revolver, nine-shot, with a blue-steel long barrel and dark wood handles. They would also seek other forensic evidence that might be available.

Using the information Chessman, Kato, and Rich had provided, the detectives proceeded to Freezette owner Robert Perry's residence, where Chessman said they had left the murder weapon. In Chessman's, Rich's, and Kato's confession—sworn and court-reported—they all asserted that Perry had given them a few bucks for the weapon. They had told Perry they needed beer money.

Perry resided on Trout River Blvd, about five minutes away from the scene of Johnnie Mae Chappell's homicide. While interviewing Perry, the detectives described the weapon to him and asked if he had received the revolver from the assailants. Perry acknowledged he had. Cody asked Perry to identify who came to his home that night with the weapon. He named each of the suspects in custody, including Davis, and he verified the date, time and described Kato's car.

"We'll have to take that revolver into custody because it is a murder weapon," Cody said.

Perry replied, "Sorry to hear that. I've sold that weapon to Deputy Sheriff William Roundtree a while back."

"You mean, Stump Roundtree?" Cody asked.

"Yeah."

The detectives went immediately to Roundtree's residence and woke him from a sound sleep. Roundtree was a dispatcher. They advised him what Perry had revealed.

"Damn," Stump said. "I sold that pistol to Blind Jim Nobles a month ago."

"Blind Jim who operates the snack stand at the Court House?" Cody asked.

"Yeah," Stump replied.

Finding Blind Jim required them to circle back to the Court House. They found Blind Jim at his snack shop, which unbelievably was only ten feet from the doors to the Sheriff's Office.

When asked about the revolver, Blind Jim said, "Yeah, I bought that pistol from Stump. I've got it right here under the counter." He reached under the counter and produced the pistol for the detectives. Ironically, the murder weapon had been languishing under Blind Jim's counter for weeks while Duval County officers, detectives, prosecutors, and judges had leaned on the counter every morning with no idea of the crucial ballistic evidence concealed within their immediate reach.

"Am I in trouble over this?" Blind Jim asked as he handed the pistol to the detectives.

Cody wrote him a receipt for the pistol. "No. The pistol was involved in a homicide, so we've got to take it. Obviously, Jim, you didn't have any way of knowing it is important evidence."

Though they did not believe that Blind Jim had any knowledge of the pistol's history, they suspected Robert Perry might have known what the weapon was used for. In his sworn confession, Rich stated that he thought they had told Perry they had shot *at* a nigger with it.

Within five minutes after taking the pistol into custody, the detectives walked a hundred feet to the property room, bagged, tagged, sealed it, and properly booked the pistol into the property room evidence locker. At the time, they did not know that the pistol, like so much other crucial evidence connected to the case, would eventually vanish or be tainted.

Chapter Five:

Conspiracy and Corruption in the Sheriff's Office and the FBI

Some explanations of a crime are not explanations:
they're part of the crime
--Olavo de Cavarlho

Sheriff John Brown always hated me
For what, I don't know:
--from Bob Marley's "I Shot the Sheriff."

Now that they had the murder weapon properly book in the evidence locker, the next logical step for the detectives would be to proceed to the county morgue to ascertain if any ballistic or other forensic evidence had been recovered. If a projectile had been retrieved from Chappell's body, in 1964 as today, ballistic examination could verify that the bullet in fact had come from Chessman's pistol.

However, because of the gravity of the situation, Sergeants Cody and Coleman decided to first go directly to Sheriff Carson to report that the evidence was overwhelming that the Chappell homicide had never been assigned for investigation. In fact, no records existed in the Duval County Sheriff's Office's investigative files recording the Chappell homicide—and in addition, the documented evidence the detectives had already obtained proved beyond all doubt that the Daily Bulletin had been intentionally altered. Only Chief Patrick had the power to alter or to order clerk John Keane to alter a Daily Bulletin entry. No legal or practical reason could explain why the Road Patrol Officer's Addendum was found hidden under Chief Patrick's chair mat—absolutely no legal reason whatever.

At this point, the detectives trusted and respected Sheriff Dale Carson, a former FBI agent. They believed he would not protect Patrick, who beyond all doubt had criminally obstructed justice in a capital Civil Rights homicide case.

Yet, they were apprehensive about approaching the sheriff because of the circumstances surrounding the Civil Service Exam for Detective Lieutenant given on July 23, 1964. After the examination had been administered and the graded results had been posted on the Civil Service bulletin board, Sergeants Claude West and Donald Coleman had the two highest scores, which qualified them for the two vacant detective lieutenant positions. However, the scores had not been visible long before Executive Secretary Louise Dorsey removed them, saying that the scores were in error and not official.

When Lieutenant Ray Headen questioned her as to why the scores were in error, Mrs. Dorsey stated that Employee Progress Reports had not been used in tabulating the final test scores. The progress reports carried a weighty 20% on the tabulated final grade. These progress reports were required by Civil Service law to be filed annually, and that in the event of a promotional exam, the most recent EPR submitted prior to the exam must be used for the tabulation of the final grade. However, it was learned that Chief Patrick had not evaluated the Detective Division employees via progress reports in over two years, in direct violation of state laws.

Two days after the test had been given and graded, the Civil Service Board directed Sheriff Carson to supply the progress reports. Sheriff Carson sent them to the board on August 6, signing them seven days after the promotional exam was given and graded. When the new results were posted, Sergeants Roland Grant and Richard Fleming were awarded the highest grades, instead of Sergeants Coleman and West. Grant and Fleming would be promoted to the rank of Detective Lieutenant upon Sheriff Carson's certification. Once Detective Coleman saw the newly posted results and requested and received a copy of the belated Employee Progress Report, he and Sergeant Cody went directly to Sheriff Carson.

The detectives advised Sheriff Carson at that time that his signature on the progress report was dated one week *after* the promotional exam had been given and graded. He was also advised that Chief Patrick and Louise Dorsey, Executive Secretary for the Civil Service Board, were the individuals responsible for producing the fraudulent and belated progress reports. The detectives pointed out that any subjective progress report that could affect the final grade of any already graded test by 20% would now allow Chief Patrick to promote whomever he pleased. Sheriff Carson listened, and said that when he directed Chief Patrick to supply the progress reports to the Civil Service Board as requested, he thought the progress reports existed and thought that Chief Patrick had simply failed to submit the reports in a timely fashion. He explained that he did not know that the reports he signed had been created after the test was given. He apologized saying, "I should have been paying closer attention to what was going on."

Sheriff Carson expressed his appreciation to the detectives for bringing the matter to his attention and vowed that he would not allow the new grades to stand, saying he certainly would not be part of such fraudulent activity. Sheriff Carson said he didn't want to be party to a criminal act and he assured the detectives he would take appropriate action to rectify the situation.

A week later, because they had not heard anything further from Sheriff Carson about the reported Civil Service fraud they had reported to him, Sergeants Cody and Coleman made inquiry as to whether the sheriff had certified the illegally promoted lieutenants, Grant and Fleming. They discovered that he had not. They then felt comfortable to go directly to the sheriff again, this time with the evidence of Chief Patrick's obstruction of justice in the Johnnie Mae Chappell homicide investigation.

Before they presented this evidence, the detectives inquired of the sheriff about the status of the Civil Service exam fraud, which they had reported to the sheriff earlier. Sheriff Carson explained that he had forwarded the forged progress report and other evidence to State Attorney William A. Hallowes, III for his evaluation. Feeling comfortable with that explanation, the detectives gave a detailed report of the obstruction they had discovered, and then furnished Sheriff Carson a copy of the altered daily bulletin, which they had obtained from the Jacksonville Police Department.

Sheriff Carson again appeared to be shocked by the revelation of Patrick's actions. The sheriff gave the detectives the same instructions that he had when they had reported the Civil Service fraud case: "Don't do anything else on this case until you hear from me." The detectives therefore went on to other work, assuming that Patrick would be immediately under the intense scrutiny of the State and Federal attorneys and FBI and probably on the way to a federal penitentiary. Because of Sheriff Carson's instructions, the detectives made no attempt on that day to approach the county medical examiner for additional ballistic evidence related to the Chappell homicide as they had earlier planned to do—if any evidence existed.

At that time, the detectives had no idea of the number and identities of the people devoted to making the Chappell case go away, but they would soon learn. And it would be one of many hard lessons for the detectives.

Chief Patrick was waiting for Cody and Coleman the next day when they came in. "You two motherfuckers come in my office." They entered. Chief Patrick's face was blood red, and he slammed the door. He stood behind his desk and exclaimed, "Let me tell you two motherfuckers something. You can't rock this fucking boat, boys, because the anchor's too fucking big. Stay out of the sheriff's office and don't touch the Chappell case again."

As Coleman and Cody left Patrick's office, Coleman said, "We're in deep shit."

Cody agreed. Cody's intuition kicked in and the realization of the implications slammed him in the gut. Cody said, "God almighty, Donald. Chief Patrick has Sheriff Carson compromised. What in the world could he have on him? Sheriff Carson obviously told Patrick what we reported to him. No one else knew."

Cody was both puzzled and infuriated. How on God's earth could Sheriff Dale Carson, a former agent of the Federal Bureau of Investigation, allow himself to become criminally complicit by obstructing justice in a racially motivated capital hate crime? Especially considering the fact that the nation was and had been in recent years replete with racial violence, homicides, church bombings and lynchings. Sheriff Carson certainly knew if it was proven that he obstructed justice by protecting the original obstructer of the Chappell homicide investigation, Chief of Detectives, James Calvin Patrick, he himself could face capital punishment.

Sergeant Cody reminded Coleman of two relevant and recent Civil Rights cases. On July 11, 1964—only a month before the detectives had solved the Chappell homicide—Lemuel Penn, a Lieutenant Colonel in the U.S. Army, who was black, had been shot to death in Colbert, Georgia by members of the Ku-Klux-Klan. Sergeants Cody and Coleman also remembered that President Johnson had to order J. Edgar Hoover to assist the local officials in Philadelphia, Mississippi, after Hoover had refused FBI involvement to locate the three young missing Civil Rights workers—Chaney, Goodman, and Schwerner. [Hoover had explained his reluctance by stating that the FBI was not a police force, but an investigative agency.] The missing three men were found on August 4, 1964, buried in a dike near Philadelphia, Mississippi. This was only a week prior to the detectives meeting with Sheriff Carson to report Chief Patrick's criminal obstruction of justice in the Chappell homicide.

Sergeant Cody continued. "Just think about it, Coleman. While a hundred and fifty plus FBI agents and 400 U.S. Naval personnel were combing Mississippi attempting to locate three missing Civil Rights workers, Chief James Calvin Patrick—an FBI Academy graduate—and his superior, Sheriff Dale George Carson—a former FBI agent—were obstructing justice in the capital murder of a black mother of ten children, a lady named Johnnie Mae Chappell."

Sergeant Coleman said, "I'm not surprised. It's like *déjà vu* for me."

Sergeant Cody replied, "What do you mean, Coleman?"

"Remember the Beverly Cochran case?"

Sergeant Cody did remember the case; however, not being directly involved in the investigation, he obviously did not know the details. Coleman then shared the story in detail.

What follows is a summary of Coleman's recollections with from an article entitled, "Dead & Buried," reported in the popular Jacksonville *Folioweekly*, April 12, 2005.

Beverly Cochran, a nineteen-year-old mother was reported as missing in February 1960. A neighbor had given detectives a description of a man seen entering her home about the time she vanished.

Duval County Sheriff's Office Detectives Donald Coleman and William Mosley, and Detective Lieutenant Ray Headen were joined by Detective Captain Jim Wingate of the City of Jacksonville Police Department. These criminal investigators had worked the Cochran case for months. After an intensive and futile search for Beverly and her abductor, a break in the case finally came. A white male in police custody bore a striking resemblance to the police artist's sketch. Emmett Spencer, a serial killer, had been arrested and convicted for the murders of several people in Florida, including two in Jacksonville. The investigating officers interviewed Spencer and an oral confession obtained.

Spencer declined to tender a written statement, citing concerns that any written confession would negatively impact current pending charges against him in Florida courts. He confessed he had abducted Beverly June Cochran at the behest of Clarence McCormick, son of Ben McCormick, one of the owners of the Jacksonville Beach construction company. The McCormick's were well respected and their company had practically built Cape Canaveral and had enjoyed extensive political influence throughout Florida.

Spencer revealed he met Clarence McCormick when they were both employed by the McCormick Construction Company. Spencer gained entry into the Cochran home and surprised Mrs. Cochran, who pleaded with him to not hurt her baby. Spencer stuffed the petite Mrs. Cochran into a duffel bag, and then transported her to Clarence McCormick waiting at the Ann-Platt Apartments at Jacksonville Beach.

The baby was left alone in the crib.

Spencer said that when they reached the apartment, McCormick broke Cochran's arms with a tire tool as she futilely attempted to fight off his advances, raped her, and then murdered her. In Spencer's confession, he related that he and McCormick then transported her body to a wooded area adjacent to Atlantic Boulevard and Mayport Road where they buried the corpse. After Spencer's confession, the detectives requested that he guide them to Beverly Cochran's house where the abduction had taken place. Though it was a dark, rainy, and foggy night, Spencer directed the detectives to the neighborhood and pointed out the exact location of the house without any difficulty. The Cochran residence was in a brand new cookie-cutter subdivision with few streetlights in which the houses all looked very much alike. From an investigative point of view, this easy identification of the house impressed the detectives. Spencer described the inside details of the house with such intricate accuracy that the detectives could only conclude he had indeed been inside the Cochran home. He drew a detailed floor plan of the home, and horribly, one that included the location of the Cochran's baby's crib. The most compelling evidentiary detail was Spencer's recollection of a red lamp with gold dragons on it positioned on a table immediately to the right as one entered the dwelling. The lamp was one that the victim's husband, James Cochran, later verified its description and location. He explained that he had obtained the lamp in Japan while in the Navy.

At this point, the detectives had no doubt about the accuracy and veracity of Spencer's detailed oral confession.

The next day, Spencer led them to the site where he claimed he and McCormick had buried Beverly's remains. Suddenly, Chief Patrick and Sheriff Carson appeared. Carson and Patrick must have been monitoring the county radio transmissions. Carson slammed on the brakes, jumped out of his car shouting, "Get that son-of-a-bitch back to Raiford! [State Penitentiary] I don't want him in my county!"

Coleman said that Chief J.C. Patrick looked directly at Coleman and flashed a cold smile.

The next day, Sheriff Carson called Sergeant Coleman to his office and ordered him to stop the investigation and he would handle the case himself. All the officers involved believed that Carson and Patrick's interference was motivated by their close friendship with the McCormick family.

Though Beverly Cochran's family begged Sheriff Carson for years to re-open the case, it was never solved nor assigned to anyone. Spencer later recanted his story, after Chief Patrick paid him a personal visit, beat him and broke his arm. According to an article in the Columbus, Georgia newspaper, Clarence McCormick was shot to death in a motel room by an individual who had participated with McCormick in several armed robberies. Emmett Spencer died in prison. Sheriff Carson and Chief Patrick maintained their friendship with the McCormick clan.

The Cochran case had taken place in 1960. Obviously, things had changed little by 1964. Coleman's story was an epiphany, a light-bulb moment for Sergeant Cody who suddenly became acutely aware of the corrupt powers he was facing.

At this point detectives Cody and Coleman both vowed at their first opportunity that they would expose Chief Patrick and Sheriff Carson's criminal obstruction of justice. They vowed this despite Chief Patrick's admonishment to not involve themselves any further in the Chappell homicide, and they were determined without really knowing how they would accomplish it. On August 28, 1964, Sergeants Cody and Coleman, due to an unbelievable circumstance and the promised help of the Federal Bureau of Investigation, thought they had the opportunity to fulfill that vow.

They were wrong.

Chapter Six:

The Sheriff and the FBI

We are a fact-gathering investigative organization only. We don't clear anybody. We don't condemn anybody
                              .—J. Edgar Hoover

You might think, 'Is this the FBI that I've seen on TV?' The difference in the myth of the FBI and the reality of the FBI is as big as the Grand Canyon.
—Ron Woods (FBI agent and United States Attorney for the Southern District of Texas)

Warren Stumph was a man with a long rap sheet and had been a frequent trustee at the Duval County Jail, which he seemed to visit frequently. Sergeant Donald Coleman had arrested Stumph on one occasion, and was surprised when Stumph called months later and asked the detective for help. Stumph was an exterminator by trade when he was not cracking safes, but said he was having a hard time finding work. Stumph said he did not want to go back to jail, but it was winter, and he did not have food, clothes or heating fuel for his family. Could Coleman do anything to help him? Sergeant Coleman took him to his church, got him blankets, food, and clothes, and even found him several exterminating jobs.

A week after Chief Patrick's eruption, which resulted in the removal of Detectives Cody and Coleman from the Chappell homicide investigation, Warren Stumph again, contacted Sergeant Coleman. This time Stumph said, "Because you were kind to me and my family and helped us, I want to do something to help you. I've got a friend who was in jail with me a while back that's now a courier in an interstate gambling ring. My friend told me there's some high-ranking officials in the Duval County Sheriff's Office and the State Attorney's Office involved in it [the gambling ring]. I've recently heard through the grapevine that Chief Patrick is out to get you and your partner—what's his name? Cody? I've decided that I'm going to help you get something on Patrick so he can't hurt you and Sergeant Cody. My friend said he'd be willing to meet with you, and as a favor to me, help any way he could. He can give you documented letters and a lot of other information. He owes me one."

Sergeant Coleman then phoned Cody and said, "I got a call from Warren Stumph, one of my informants, and he wants to meet with us."

"What does he want?" Sergeant Cody asked.

Coleman filled Cody in on how he had arrested and then later helped Stumph out. After they talked about Stump's phone call, they thought this might be the chance they needed if Sheriff Carson and Chief Patrick were two of the high-ranking officials Stumph's friend had alluded to. Because of their powerful positions, an interstate gambling ring seemed like something Patrick and Carson and members of the State Attorney's Office could be part of. Sergeant Coleman phoned Stumph to find out how they could set up a meeting and find out more about his friend, his allegations, and his offer to help. Cody was eager to meet Stumph.

After they talked, Stumph agreed to a meeting. At the meeting, Stumph told Sergeants Coleman and Cody that they could meet Stumph's former cellmate that very Sunday.

"Where can we meet him and how will we know him?" Sergeant Cody asked.

Stumph said, "Every Sunday he books a room at Slappy's Motel in Jax and makes a drop or picks up money. He gets there around one o'clock usually. You'll know him when you see him. He drives a cream-colored Chrysler with South Carolina tags."

"We can't meet him this Sunday, but see if you can arrange something for the next week," Cody said. "You say he's there every week?"

"Every week," Stumph said.

Slappy's was a tourist court motel and a well-known trysting place in North Jacksonville on Highway 17. They thought that would be a likely place someone who wanted to maintain a low profile would choose.

The detectives immediately contacted the FBI since the interstate gambling Stumph had described was a federal offense. An agent named Robert J. McCarthy was dispatched to meet with the two detectives. The detectives, suspicious of the veracity of Stumph's allegations, related to Agent McCarthy Stumph's claims and suggested Agent McCarthy stake out Slappy's and see if he could identify the male subject and vehicle bearing a South Carolina tag, which Stumph had described. Agent McCarthy agreed that Stumph's claims merited investigation.

So, the following Sunday, Agent McCarthy staked out the motel and remained until dark and did not observe a man or vehicle matching Stumph's furnished description. That night Agent McCarthy contacted Sergeant Cody and related he had not observed a vehicle of that description anywhere near the motel. Agent McCarthy exchanged phone numbers with sergeants Cody and Coleman and told the detectives to call him at home if they needed to in case anything new developed. Cody thanked him and said that if they heard any more from informant Stumph they would let him know.

Stumph contacted Sergeant Coleman the next day and said that his "friend," whom he now identified as Joe, had decided to relocate on Sunday and was now in Room 404 at the Crown Hotel on the corner of Main and Ashley streets. This seedy hotel was above a bar, and was known to be a hangout for whores, dope fiends, and pimps. The detectives thought this might explain why Agent McCarthy did not see the suspect on Sunday. Stumph said that his friend still wanted them to meet him in his room at the new location.

"No," Sergeant Coleman said. "Tell your man that Sergeant Cody and I will meet him at the fountain plaza where the swans are in front of Ivy's department store, across the street from his hotel."

As he hung up the phone, Sergeant Coleman thought he heard Stumph whisper, "*It's a frame. It's a frame.*" Sergeant Coleman called Sergeant Cody at home. "I thought I heard Stumph whisper that this meeting was a frame. At least that's what it sounded like."

Sergeant Cody had a bad feeling. He said, "I'm going to call Agent McCarthy again."

As it was on the weekend, Cody called McCarthy at home, filled him in on the new developments and asked him to meet with them again. McCarthy agreed. Cody also called Sergeant Claude West, an officer they trusted who could be a witness, and Cody and West met McCarthy at what was then the riverfront adjacent to the Seaboard Coastline Railway Headquarters [That rail line is now named the CSX].

When Agent McCarthy arrived, Sergeant Cody filled Agent McCarthy in on Stumph's second call and his friend's new hotel location and said they didn't know for sure what was going on, but the detectives were deeply concerned and wanted Agent McCarthy to be a witness to the arranged meeting to take place at Ivey's Plaza.

The FBI agent and detectives drove to a location near the Crown Hotel and parked, then walked west toward the designated meeting place. On the way, they passed a parking lot behind the Crown Hotel where they noticed a light colored four-door sedan that looked suspiciously like a police or official vehicle. The automobile was a late model Ford, much newer and in better condition than the cars around it. The car bore a Florida 25- tag, which indicated the vehicle, was registered in Jackson County Florida. Agent McCarthy recorded the tag number in his notebook. The trio then proceeded to Ivey's Department store. Upon arrival, Sergeants Cody, and West and Agent McCarthy positioned themselves inside the main glass entrance to the plaza. This afforded them a clear view of the fountain where the meeting was to take place.

At 1:00 p.m., the agreed upon time, Sergeant Coleman approached the fountain. At the same time, a tall and rather seedy looking raw-boned white male, dressed in rumpled shirt and slacks, approached the fountain from the opposite direction and addressed Coleman. The pair talked several minutes, and then the man turned and walked towards the Crown Hotel.

Sergeant Cody said to West and McCarthy, "Stay put. I'm going to follow that man and see where's he headed." Sergeant Cody followed the male subject and observed him entering the Crown Hotel. Nearing the hotel entrance, Sergeant Cody observed the same yet unidentified white male in a public phone booth near the hotel entrance. Sergeant Cody returned to plaza outside Ivey's, rejoining Agent McCarthy and Sergeants West and Coleman by the fountain.

According to Sergeant Coleman, the man approached and said, "Are you Coleman?"

"Yes," Coleman said.

"Where's Cody?" the man asked.

"He's busy."

"Well, I'm Joe Johnson, and I've got the forged documents you were asking for."

Sergeant Coleman said, "I don't know what forged documents you are talking about. This is the first I've heard about forged documents. I'm only here because of information provided me by a reliable informant, Warren Stumph. Stumph said that he had been incarcerated with you and that you owed him a big favor. Stumph said you were involved in an interstate gambling ring and that you were willing to furnish documented records that would implicate high ranking officers in the Duval Sheriff's Office as well as members of the State Attorney's Office."

Joe seemed surprised and confused.

Sergeant Coleman said, "If you try to furnish me any falsified or forged documents, I will immediately place your ass in the Duval County Jail."

Joe turned to leave and said, "I'm relocating. If you change your mind, you can contact me tonight at the Seminole hotel downtown."

When Agent McCarthy heard Coleman's account of the meeting, he said, "What in the world do you officers think is going on?"

Sergeant Cody replied, "We don't know for sure, but we can only surmise that Sheriff Carson or Chief Patrick or both are somehow behind this. It's obvious someone wants to falsely incriminate us."

"Why would either of them want to frame you?" McCarthy asked.

The detectives explained to Agent McCarthy that they had incontrovertible evidence that last March, Chief Patrick, with Carson's knowledge, had successfully and intentionally criminally obstructed justice in the homicide investigation of the murder of Johnnie Mae Chappell, a black female. They related how only a few days ago they had communicated Patrick's criminal activity to Sheriff Carson, but it had become evident that, instead of seeking Patrick's prosecution, Carson had chosen to protect Patrick and conceal his actions, and by doing so, Carson was himself obstructing justice and complicit in the cover-up.

Agent McCarthy appeared to be in total shock, especially since he knew that Sheriff Carson had been a former FBI agent.

Before Agent McCarthy left them, the detectives strongly expressed their belief that the unidentified "Joe" was a special agent of the Florida Sheriff's Bureau brought to Jacksonville to assist Sheriff Carson and others in an effort to frame the detectives.

Later, the detectives would learn they were more right about "Joe" than they suspected.

Agent McCarthy replied that he would be in touch with the detectives as soon as he completed his reports and related to his superiors what had happened. Cody, West, and Coleman expected Agent McCarthy to make a full objective report and that justice would now, without a doubt, quickly be administered. Sergeants Cody, West, and Coleman were confident in the FBI's integrity and they believed the FBI would immediately initiate a full-scale criminal investigation.

On the other hand, the detectives had some doubts. They remembered that Sheriff Carson worked under the direct supervision of D.K. Brown, the current Special Agent in charge of the Jacksonville FBI office. These apprehensions later proved to be well founded.

On the same day of the meeting with "Joe," Detectives Cody and Coleman still assigned to the four to twelve shift, still trying to make some sense of recent events, contacted Sheriff Carson at his home and asked him to meet with them. Carson said they should meet him at Hargrave's Steak House in Riverside near the Five Points area. Sheriff Carson said he would be at the restaurant around 7:00 p.m.

The detectives met Sheriff Carson at the restaurant as directed. Not long after they sat down, Sheriff William Whitehead from Union County sauntered in. Like Carson, he was a powerful and politically influential man in Florida, and Sheriff Carson's close personal friend. Seeing him at that particular place and time seemed to be just too much of a coincidence. When Sheriff Whitehead passed Carson, he nodded, moved on and sat at a table alone. The detectives assumed that he must have been there as a witness for Carson in case anything went south. Close, intimate friends don't just pass each other in a restaurant and not speak. Later, the facts would make it apparent that he was indeed there as a witness (or backup) to Carson's meeting with the detectives.

The detectives then related to Sheriff Carson what had happened that day.

Sergeant Cody asked Sheriff Carson, "Sheriff, do you know what is going on here? Do you have any firsthand, personal knowledge about the events I've related?"

Sheriff Carson denied any knowledge of what had occurred at Ivey's Plaza.

The detectives were starting to clearly understand the fact that corrupt politicians and officials all operated by a philosophy of "Deny, deny, and deny." They did not know yet that this philosophy also included, "And then kill the messengers."

Sheriff Carson wanted to appear cooperative, so he agreed to accompany Sergeants Cody and Coleman to the Seminole Hotel in downtown Jacksonville to confront and question the mysterious "Joe."

Upon arrival, the trio learned from the desk clerk that there was a man named Joe Johnson registered in the hotel. The detectives and Sheriff Carson proceeded to the man's room. When this "Joe Johnson" opened the door, the detectives immediately advised Sheriff Carson that this was not the man they had met at Ivey's Plaza. The man stepped outside the room and closed the door. The detectives identified themselves and said they were conducting an investigation, looking for a man known as Joe Johnson, but it was obvious that he was not the man they were attempting to locate.

The man said, "There's not going to be a report filed on this, is there? I hope not, because the lady in there is not my wife."

The detectives told him to not worry and that his party could continue.

Sergeant Cody wondered what the odds were for finding two men using the same alias on the same day. One, obviously a man screwing around on his wife, and the other, not so obviously connected with Sheriff Carson in a criminal act.

The detectives told Sheriff Carson that they would contact him if they received any more information, and Sheriff Carson responded in kind. The sheriff left and the detectives returned to their four to twelve shift duties.

After his shift ended that night, Sergeant Cody drove to Mariana, Florida in Jackson County with the mysterious Joe's tag number in hand. Cody ran the 25-license plate number, and the Jackson County records revealed that Joe's vehicle was indeed a state-owned vehicle assigned to the Florida Sheriff's Bureau, which made it obvious beyond all doubt that the mysterious Joe was a special agent for the Florida Sheriff's Bureau.

Sergeants Cody and Coleman knew that the only individual who had the authority to involve and summon an agent from the Florida Sheriff's Bureau to Duval County was Sheriff Dale Carson. The governor could not do it; even the President of the United States could not do it. Only Sheriff Dale Carson could do it.

*   *   *

It was not until much later that the detectives learned the true identify of Joe Johnson. His name was actually Joe Townsend, and his story is told in a sworn deposition court reported on April 23, 1982. Townsend was sixty-five at the time of the deposition.

Joe R. Townsend was at one point in his career a trained polygrapher and special investigator for the Office of Special Investigations (OSI) located in Washington, D.C. After his retirement, Townsend was hired by the Florida Sheriff's Bureau.

In his deposition, Townsend explains how the Florida Sheriff's Bureau worked. He said that a sheriff needing assistance would call the bureau director and request it. Perry Ivie, Townsend's immediate supervisor, directed Townsend to participate in an undercover assignment. He was to appear in Duval County as a "crumb bumb" in old clothes. Ivie said that Duval County had a situation that required someone not known in that area. Townsend had never been to Jacksonville before, so he was a good match. Townsend was directed to not contact anyone but Sheriff Carson.

Townsend attested that he met Sheriff Carson by an abandoned hangar at old Imeson Airport north of Jacksonville. They sat in Carson's Chrysler convertible and talked. Townsend thought it unusual that a sheriff would be utilizing a convertible as a police vehicle. Sheriff Carson told Townsend that he had received information through informants that two Duval County detectives, Sergeants Cody and Coleman, were attempting to obtain forged documents that would implicate other officers and officials in graft, kickbacks, payoffs, and particularly interstate gambling. Sheriff Carson requested Townsend to stay in a fleabag hotel, the Crown (not Slappy's as Stumph first said), and to dress like a tramp. Townsend was to meet with the detectives and sell them documents.

In the deposition, Townsend reveals the fact that Sheriff Carson had arranged for the State Attorney's office to compile the false documents that were to be presented to the detectives. (Is this not an example of Criminal Conspiracy 101? You bet!)

Townsend was given a cover story. He was to present himself as a recently released convict out of Tennessee who had served time for forgery. Townsend was to offer to obtain forged official documents for Detectives Coleman and Cody. At that point, Townsend assumed he would be working undercover to expose and nail the kind of men he most detested—crooked cops.

When Townsend met Coleman, he followed Carson's instructions and told the detective that he had been informed that Coleman and Cody wanted to obtain forged documents which would implicate individuals in the Duval County Sheriff's Office and State Attorney's Office, and that he was in a position to furnish the detectives with such documents.

Townsend asked Sergeant Coleman what information he wanted the documents to contain. Townsend said that instead of accepting his offer, the surprised Sergeant Coleman began to question him. Townsend says in his deposition: "Coleman, in no uncertain terms told me he would put my ass in jail if I gave him false documents. The meeting was, I should say, abruptly ended. After that he told me he didn't want anything I had unless it was true in fact."

Townsend said he left and went to a payphone, called Sheriff Dale Carson and advised him what had happened. Sheriff Carson replied, "Well, if that is the case, it has been blown. You had better go back to Chipley [Townsend's city of residence in Jackson County]."

Therefore, it is crystal clear that after their meeting at the steakhouse, when Sheriff Carson went with Coleman and Cody to check out the mysterious Joe Johnson at the Seminole Hotel as was mentioned earlier, Sheriff Dale Carson already knew the true identity of Joe Johnson (Townsend) and that he had already departed as instructed.

Chapter Seven:

"Don't call me again . . ."

Politics, in a sense, has always been a con game.
—Joe McGinnis

When they had parted at the site of the original sting, Agent McCarthy seemed, as stated earlier, appalled, shocked and just plain overwhelmed at what he had just learned and observed.

The next day, as agreed, Agent McCarthy contacted Detective Cody by telephone at his home about 10:00 a.m. Sergeant Claude West monitored the call on Cody's home extension. The agent said in a quivering voice, "Lee, this is Agent Bob McCarthy. I just left D.K. Brown's office. D. K. Brown [Special Agent in Charge in Jacksonville] told me that if I ever even spoke to you, Sergeant Coleman, or West again, I would be censured and transferred. So please, for God's sake, Lee, please don't any of you ever call or contact me again. I have children you know." Then he abruptly hung up the phone.

Sergeants Cody, West, and Coleman never heard from Agent McCarthy or any other FBI representative regarding the criminal conduct they observed and reported.

Sergeant Cody had been expecting a call from FBI Agent McCarthy requesting that he and Sergeants Coleman and West come to the Jacksonville FBI office or U.S. Attorney's Office. Instead, the agent who had been assigned to assist them had now himself become a victim of the deep-seated corruption. Moreover, that night when their shift began, as usual the detectives entered Chief Patrick's office to get their car keys, flashlights, and radios. There in plain sight, the detectives observed on Patrick's desk a notepad, with this written clearly on it: CROWN HOTEL, ROOM 404. The detectives knew from that note that Chief Patrick was involved in the sting along with Sheriff Carson. Did a drunken Chief J.C. Patrick leave the note accidentally in plain sight? On the other hand, was it intentionally left visible to the detectives, knowing that the eyes of a trained detective would immediately notice it? The detectives questioned in their minds if this could be another setup, wondering if Chief Patrick would return after the detectives left the Sheriff's office to see if anything had again been removed from his desk. They noticed that the note was still there when they came in at midnight to end their shift.

At this point, it was now woefully apparent to the detectives that Chief Patrick, Sheriff Carson, State Attorney Hallowes III, and FBI Special Agent in Charge D.K. Brown were all on the same page. In addition, a part of the page's contents can be found in the Criminal Statutes of the State of Florida, dealing with compounding a felony in chapter 843.13, which reads as follows:

Whoever, having knowledge of the commission of an offense punishable with death or by imprisonment in the state prison, takes money or a gratuity or reward, or an engagement thereof, upon an agreement or understanding, expressed or implied, to compound or conceal such offense, or not to prosecute thereof, or not to give evidence thereof, shall when such offense of which he or she has knowledge is punishable with death or imprisonment in the state prison for life, be guilty of a felony of the third degree.

Another portion of that page can be found in subsection one of the Fourteenth Amendment to our nation's Constitution, which reads as follows:

Each state shall guarantee every citizen under their jurisdiction equal protection of the laws.

Unfortunately for Detectives Cody and Coleman, men in power who are guilty of such criminality not only can compound a felony and deny one his or her Constitutional rights, and as mentioned earlier, such men also consistently follow the philosophy of this old adage: *Deny, deny, deny, and then kill the messenger.*

To most people, even to those in law enforcement, the reputation of the Federal Bureau of Investigation was stellar. The FBI never gave up on a case, its agents were above corruption, and no one would be immune from prosecution. If the detectives held any such beliefs of the FBI in their hearts, they would soon learn that these perceptions were not well founded. Nor would the FBI prove to be interested in exposing the corruption and obstruction of justice in Duval County. This will be obvious, especially when one takes a close look at D.K. Brown, the Special Agent in Charge of the Jacksonville Bureau of Federal Investigation.

Immediately after Jacksonville consolidation, D.K. Brown retired from the FBI and in March of 1968, Jacksonville mayor Hans G. Tanzler appointed D.K. Brown chief of the newly reorganized Jacksonville Sheriff's Office. A March 22, 1968 article in the *Times Union* says, "Brown's appointment was being made with the full consent of Sheriff (Dale) Carson." Carson himself said about Brown's appointment that it "was the next best thing to getting J. Edgar [Hoover] himself."

D.K. Brown, who in 1967 received the FBI's "outstanding performance" rating, was according to Hans

G. Tanzler, expected to "restore confidence and to refurbish the department from top to bottom."

This endorsement by Tanzler is significant. Tanzler was formerly a criminal court judge, was now serving as Mayor of the new consolidated city of Jacksonville, and viewed as a pillar of justice. He was so hard on criminals that he was known as "Father Time." In 1964, Detectives Cody and Coleman met with Tanzler to seek his assistance in their desperate search for justice. After the detectives revealed to him the criminal activity they had uncovered, Tanzler looked at his watch and said, "I'm sorry. I've got a lunch appointment I must attend. But before I leave, let me give you two officers some sound advice: You're fooling with some vicious bastards and you better watch your back."

Apparently, D.K. Brown was one of those vicious bastards he spoke of. Was D.K. Brown's appointment to this new Jacksonville post just coincidental? Would Brown have been appointed had Brown nailed Sheriff Carson when he had the opportunity, sworn duty, and inescapable legal obligation to do so? Or was D.K. Brown's new prestigious position as chief of the Jacksonville Sheriff's Office (JSO) actually a reward from Sheriff Carson for Brown's part in covering up the vindictive agenda against the detectives and the cover-up of the civil rights violations against Johnnie Mae Chappell? What was it worth to Sheriff Carson in order to escape detection and/or detention? Whatever the explanation may be, these officials clearly violated their sworn oath of office. As clearly stated in Florida Criminal Statute 843.14, the law makes it clear that when one assists a felonious individual or individuals to avoid or escape detention and or detection, he or she becomes a principal in the crime.

The fact that the Jacksonville FBI Office failed in its duties was even more discouraging to Sergeant Cody.

Later, pursuing the rights provided by the freedom of Information Act, Detective Cody's research revealed that not one word in the FBI national archives contained any reference to the names of Johnnie Mae Chappell or Detectives C. Lee Cody, Donald R. Coleman or Claude R. West.

Years later, Detective Cody contacted Agent McCarthy at McCarthy's new post in the Midwest. He advised him that he [Cody] and others had initiated a Civil Rights lawsuit against Sheriff Carson for violating their 14th Amendment Civil Rights and they would respectfully request that McCarthy testify in their case about the events that transpired at Ivey's Plaza, regarding the attempt of Sheriff Carson and State Attorney Hallowes to falsely incriminate Cody and Coleman. Sergeant Cody asked McCarthy, "Do you recall D.K. Brown's threat after you reported the criminal acts you had witnessed at Ivey's Plaza?"

McCarthy's reply was terse and immediate. "I don't recall my being present at Ivey's Plaza or D.K. Brown's threatening me."

"Let me remind you what you told me." Sergeant Cody repeated what had happened and what had been said and how D.K. Brown (Special Agent in Charge) had threatened McCarthy with censure and transfer if he pursue the case any further or spoke to any of the detectives again.

McCarthy repeated, "D.K. Brown did not threaten me."

"Don't take this to your grave, Bob. You know very well that Detectives Coleman, West, and I can prove beyond all doubt that you were at Ivey's and you were a forewarned eyewitness to a crime that violated our Civil Rights. You were given information to begin a prosecution. Had the FBI followed through on your testimony and report, Sheriff Carson and others would have been prosecuted. Your office had to have covered it up or a report would have been generated. Did you write one, Bob?"

"Well, I don't know. It was so long ago . . . ."

"Well, is right," Sergeant Cody said. "We're ready to hit the polygraph. We hope you are." Agent McCarthy abruptly hung up the phone again. Apparently, in Agent McCarthy's mind, it was like the incident at the Crown Hotel and Ivey's Plaza had never happened. Cody knew that McCarthy probably had only a few years left before retirement. He wondered if there were any other ghosts or closeted skeletons McCarthy would be leaving behind once he left the FBI. Can one live with denial so long that a distorted history actually becomes truth in one's mind?

To address the larger question, why did D.K. Brown not allow the FBI to act on Agent McCarthy's reported eye-witnessed criminal activity? Was it to protect his former subordinate and close personal friend, Sheriff Dale Carson and to ensure his future employment with the Jacksonville Sheriff's Office?

Sure it was.

As previously mentioned, before he came to Jacksonville, D.K. Brown had worked in Los Angeles, in what was considered the number three position for the FBI in the country. The only higher ranking and more prestigious positions were those of Deputy Director Clyde Tolson and Director, J. Edgar Hoover.

D.K. Brown was getting on in years and nearing retirement, so he came to Jacksonville, a far less strenuous position, in order to complete his tenure of duty. He was a Mormon by faith and according to rumors, considered a top man in the FBI, on the short list for the director's job, if and when Hoover retired.

Facing such power, had he objected to D.K. Brown's obstruction of justice, Agent McCarthy would have surely seen D.K. Brown's threats carried out and his career go down the toilet.

*   *   *

It is important here to relate the events escalating Sheriff Dale Carson's rise to power. A few years before Carson, Rex Sweat, a Florida icon, was elected Sheriff of Duval County and served twenty-five years. Sheriff Sweat had a dark side that eventually caught up with him and he was defeated by Al Cahill, an insurance executive, who ran on a reform platform, claiming he would clean up the Sheriff's Office and rid Duval County of corruption. However, within a period of two years, Al Cahill realized he had taken over a criminal enterprise that Sweat had managed for well over twenty years. Cahill was not as efficient as Rex Sweat in the management of a criminal enterprise and so soon found himself embroiled in all kinds of legal troubles.

Ironically, Sergeant Claude West, a witness of the events at Ivey's Plaza and one of Sheriff Dale Carson's future victims, was the deputy sheriff who supplied the information to Governor Leroy Collins that ultimately caused the removal of Sheriff Cahill. Sadly, Sergeant West's second attempt to rid Duval County of a corrupt sheriff (Dale Carson) would be less successful.

However, history has revealed that often one problem can be removed in the political arena only to be replaced by a worse one. After Al Cahill was removed from office, Governor Leroy Collins appointed Dale Carson as

57

Sheriff of Duval County. Carson left the FBI, served his appointment term, and then publicly ran for office of the Sheriff in 1960 and was elected.

Sheriff Carson would attend national FBI fraternal meetings with D.K. Brown and Chief of Detectives James Calvin Patrick, himself a graduate of the FBI Academy in Washington D.C. Sheriff Carson and Patrick were known to be close friends, but there was another issue that makes Chief Patrick significant. As powerful as Sheriff Carson was, he also had some weaknesses. One of those weaknesses could have become a fatal flaw. Not long after his election in 1960, Sheriff Carson's Chief of Detectives placed an anchor around Carson's neck that threatened to drag him down—a weight heavy enough that it allowed Chief Patrick to manipulate and control Sheriff Carson at will.

Let's just say her name is Margaret, a former employee of the Sheriff's office. According to a sworn, notarized affidavit, furnished to Sergeant Cody from an official in the Duval County Sheriff's Office, Margaret had been intimate with someone in the Sheriff's Office, and she found herself pregnant. According to this affidavit in Cody's possession, in order to handle the delicate matter of this pregnancy, Chief of Detectives Patrick and Vice Squad Chief Hamlin, at the behest of Sheriff Dale Carson, transported this young lady to Patrick's mother's home in Atlanta, Georgia, located at 717 University Avenue N.W., where she received medical attention from a Dr. Allen. According to her grandson, J.C. Patrick Jr., Imo Wilbanks Patrick, the Chief's mother, had experience assisting as midwife.

Now understand, in the 1960's, this action was a very serious crime of the first magnitude, a federal violation of the Mann Act, which forbade the transportation of a female across state lines for immoral purposes. In those days, Sergeant Cody says, you would have received less time for shooting the President of the United States. Chief Patrick's offered and accepted assistance was an obvious chokehold on Sheriff Carson. After learning of this criminal activity, Detectives Cody, Coleman, and West and others understood how Chief Patrick had repeatedly compromised and manipulated Sheriff Dale Carson. The meaning of Chief Patrick's earlier words, "You can't rock this boat, boys, because the anchor is too fucking big," became as clear as Arctic ice.

A conversation Sergeant Cody had with Margaret not long after her Atlanta trip also took on a greater significance. Cody was still a uniformed officer at the time. After she had left the employment of the Sheriff's Office, Margaret had given an open invitation to officers in the DSO (Duval County Sheriff's Office) to stop in for coffee should they be in her neighborhood. One night, Officer Cody and his partner Earl Taylor stopped to have coffee with Margaret and her mother in Margaret's new mobile home, which was located on Beat One, which included the area along U.S. Highway 17 North.

As they drank their coffee, Cody, just trying to make conversation, asked, "Margaret, where in the world did you get this beautiful new mobile house?"

She winked and said, "The Sheriff bought it for me."

"Yeah, sure he did," Officer Cody said. "Why would he do that?"

With a big smile, Margaret said, "Because I got him in the bag, Lee."

The officers drank their coffee and left. Cody pondered her statement about having the sheriff in the bag for many years. Now, Sergeant Cody is sure Margaret was not joking with him at all about how she obtained the fine new mobile home.

The Jacksonville *FolioWeekly* constructed a blistering expose of Sheriff Dale Carson, entitled "Meet the Sheriff," which they published in April 2006. Before the article's publication, an investigative reporter for the magazine contacted Margaret and confronted her with the previously mentioned affidavit that detailed her and Chief Patrick's trip to Atlanta. When confronted with the contents of that affidavit, Margaret became very emotional and said, "Oh, my God! I thought all the horror at the Sheriff's Office was forever behind me."

After learning the details of her full story and because they thought she had suffered enough, the *Folio* elected to not include her name and story in the magazine's expose.

Unfortunately, for Margaret and for many others who had been victimized by Sheriff Dale Carson and his cronies, the horror was far from over and would ever linger.

Cody often reflects back on this young employee of the Sheriff's Office and thinks about what a kind and generous personality this young lady possessed. Even today, it angers Sergeant Cody to think of how men like Sheriff Carson and Chief Patrick took advantage of her.

*   *   *

A series of later incidents were also bad omens for Sergeants Cody and Coleman and these events foreshadowed the hurricane brewing on the horizon of the detectives' careers. One focal point was the already discussed Civil Service exam for Detective Lieutenant. Not hearing anything regarding the illegal promotions or of Chief Patrick's obstruction of justice, the detectives made inquiry and learned that on August 19, Sheriff Carson had certified the promotion of Sergeants Fleming and Grant to Detective Lieutenant. The future careers of Sergeants Cody and Coleman were thus literally and prophetically written on the wall.

Other incidents bade doom for the detectives. In the spring of 1965, Sergeants Cody and Coleman were seated in criminal court on the front pew, waiting for their case to be called. At that time there was a catwalk, a walkway that connected the county jail to the courthouse with several holding cells to secure prisoners until they were ready to appear before the judge. Through that walkway that day passed a convicted felon named Ronald Edward Roberts, whose preferred criminal activities were armed robbery and auto theft. Roberts recognized Detectives Cody and Coleman and nodded as he walked by them. Though it may seem surprising and ironic, in this case, and as often happened in contrast to popular belief, often no animosity existed between the criminal element and police officers, especially if the officers were known to be fair and were not brutal or verbally abusive.

As detectives, Cody and Coleman had made it their business to know who the criminals in Duval County were and what business they were in. Roberts had a heavy rap sheet and the detectives had interviewed him as a suspect in a robbery not long ago.

A few minutes later, the bailiff appeared and said, "Sergeant Cody? Sergeant Coleman? Mr. Roberts in the holding cell would like to speak to you two officers."

After their courtroom duties, the detectives went to the holding cell. Cody said, "What's up, Ronnie? The Bailiff said you wanted to speak to us."

Roberts nodded. "Yeah, I do. I was just extradited from Georgia back to Florida on a fugitive warrant, when something unusual happened in the county jail, and I wanted to ask you about it. What in the fuck have you guys done?"

"Why in the world would you ask that?" Cody asked. It seemed to him that too many people were asking them this same question. He had a feeling he already knew the answer.

Roberts continued. "Yesterday, I was taken from the county jail by two county detectives—one named Suber and one named Touchton—to Chief Patrick's office. Patrick asked me to be seated. After they took my handcuffs off, Patrick placed his revolver on his desk. That really frightened me. When Patrick ordered the other two detectives who brought me there to leave the room and shut the door, I fully realized that I was alone in the room with Chief Patrick and no other witnesses, and if he chose to, it would be easy for him to shoot me and swear that I reached for his service revolver and that he only shot me to protect himself.

"Patrick then proceeded to inform me that he could see to it that I never did a day's time for the offense for which I was under arrest. Chief Patrick wanted me to testify under oath that you and Sergeant Coleman arrested me on an outstanding fugitive warrant and instead of booking me, you released me. Chief Patrick said he was acting on behalf of Sheriff Carson. He made all kinds of other promises, too. He said they would wipe my slate clean if I helped him. I told Chief Patrick, no. I wouldn't lie for him or the Sheriff."

"What happened when you said *no*?" Sergeant Cody asked.

"Chief Patrick called the detectives outside his office who had brought me over from the jail and told them, 'Get in here and get that son of a bitch out of here.

62

Put him in solitaire. Maybe that'll change his mind.' And that's what they did."

In 1982, when the detectives filed their Civil Rights lawsuit in Federal Court, Cody and Attorney Carol Cayer traveled to the Florida Federal Correctional Institution to interview Ronnie Roberts. During the interview, Roberts reaffirmed what he had told Sergeants Coleman and Cody previously in the Duval County courthouse.

Chapter Eight:
And the Frames Go On . . .

We are not permitted to choose the frame of our
destiny. But what we put into it is ours.
—Dag Hammarskjold, Swedish Statesman.

Sheriff Carson, Chief Patrick and their cronies continued their very earnest and determined conspiratorial campaign to end the careers and meddlesome influence of Sergeants Cody, Coleman, and West as well as Lieutenant Ray Headen, whose only involvement was his open sympathy for their quest for justice and his open criticism of Sheriff Carson's corrupt practices.

As previously delineated in an earlier chapter, Sheriff Carson's campaign against the detectives had started with the trouble surrounding the mysterious Joe Townsend (August 1964), which was followed by the attempted recruitment of convicted felon Ronnie Roberts (September 1964). Sheriff Carson, Chief Patrick, and their conspiratorial accomplice Fourth Judicial Attorney William A. Hallowes III continued to look for ways and people to use to frame and discredit Sergeants Cody and Coleman. The Chief and Sheriff expanded their conspiratorial efforts by now targeting two other criminals whom Cody and Coleman had previously arrested.

The first case involved a petty officer in the Navy. The detectives were dispatched to the scene of a rape. The woman that met them at the door was calm, but the detectives could tell that she appeared to be in shock and in utter disbelief at what had happened.

The detectives introduced themselves. She said, "You won't have to do much investigating because the man who raped me was a shipmate and best friend of my husband. She furnished his name, the description of the clothing he was wearing, the automobile he drove, and where he lived. Then, because she was in no shape emotionally to be driving, the detectives called an ambulance and transported her to the Duval Medical Center, the county hospital, to be tested for spermatozoa and physical trauma.

Sergeants Cody and Coleman proceeded to the address of the alleged perpetrator, arriving within forty-five minutes of the reported rape. The car the victim described was parked in the driveway. On the way to the door, the detectives touched the hood of the car. It was warm, indicating it had recently been driven. They knocked on the door and were met by a young white male who fit the description the victim had given. They asked if they could come in and the man said they could.

The detectives advised the man why they were there. The man said, "Well, I'm not surprised."

The suspect's wife was home at the time. Naturally, she was upset at the presence of the detectives and wanted to know what was happening. The detectives tactfully told her that they had some business with her husband at the Sheriff's Office and she could talk to him later.

The detectives asked the man to dress himself and accompany them to the Sheriff's Office, to which he agreed. When the detectives followed the man into the bedroom, the detectives observed hanging on the poster bed the clothes that exactly matched the clothes the victim had described her assailant as wearing. Fortunately, for the detectives, the man dressed in those same clothes, which might be needed for evidence later.

As the man wasn't under arrest at this point, they didn't cuff him. En route to the Sheriff's Office, the suspect stated, "Officers, it looks like I really fucked up this time."

Sergeant Cody said, "Well, the reason you're in this car with us is because your best friend's wife accused you of rape, and we've got to get to the bottom of it, son."

"Well, I did it, and I'm so ashamed."

Upon hearing this oral confession, Sergeant Cody said, "You are now under arrest." The detectives pulled over to the side of the road and asked him to step out. They patted him down, advised him to seek legal counsel, handcuffed him and returned him to the vehicle.

The detectives placed the suspect in the county jail, took his clothes into evidence, and then contacted the hospital personnel who informed them that the woman had tested positive for spermatozoa.

The detectives decided to not attempt to elicit a sworn confession from the suspect because they felt the already provided oral confession, physical evidence, and victim's testimony would be more than sufficient for prosecution and conviction. In addition, their experience dictated that a competent attorney could sometimes use a written confession to prosecutorial disadvantage. This was especially true since the landmark Supreme Court case, *Escobedo vs. State of Illinois*; (June 1964) had just been decided. Because of this Supreme Court ruling, written confessions had to follow very specific and complicated guidelines and the detectives were concerned that the case might be placed in jeopardy. That ruling held:

Where the investigation is no longer a general inquiry into unsolved crime but has begun to focus upon particular suspect, the suspect has been taken into police custody, the police carry out process of interrogations that lends itself to eliciting incriminating statements, suspect has requested and been denied opportunity to consult with his lawyer, and police have not effectively warned him of his absolute constitutional right to remain silent, the accused has been denied assistance of counsel in violation of Sixth Amendment as made obligatory upon the states by Fourteenth Amendment, and no statement elicited by police during interrogation may be used against him at criminal trial.

As the reader can see from even a casual read of this ruling, the concerns of the detectives were well founded.

The detectives went to the hospital the next day, interviewed the doctor who examined the victim, and retrieved her medical report.

When the defendant went to trial, he was convicted. When Sergeant Cody and Sergeant Coleman were testifying, they both noticed Chief Patrick in the courtroom. Patrick had never monitored or observed the detectives in court before, so after all they had already been through, they knew Chief Patrick and Sheriff Carson had something else up their sleeves and were likely gathering information for another frame attempt.

The detectives found out what Sheriff Carson and Chief Patrick were up to very soon thereafter. Not long afterward, within a week in fact, upon entering the Sheriff's office, the detectives observed Perry Ivie, a special agent and polygrapher for the Florida Sheriff's Bureau.

The detectives recognized the man, and had actually met him before, but they did not know he was Florida Sheriff's Bureau Special Agent Joe Townsend's supervisor, the mysterious Joe at the Crown Hotel. Agent Ivie was standing by one of the interrogation rooms and motioned for the detectives to come to him. As previously mentioned, the detectives knew that the only person who could request personnel assistance from the Florida Sheriff's Bureau would be Sheriff Carson, so they assumed this was not a good omen.

"Step inside," Ivie said. When he had closed the door, he said, "What the hell have you guys done?"

Same old song, different day, Cody thought. "Well, Perry, why would you ask that?"

Agent Ivie said, "Well, let me tell you what has gone on. Sheriff Carson requested my presence in Jacksonville and said that he had two detectives that testified in a rape trial. The suspect, they claimed, had made an oral confession, and Carson said he had reason to believe that the detectives had perjured themselves and that the suspect had not made that oral confession.

"I found this reasoning strange, if for no other reason than the fact that the suspect had already been found guilty as charged in court on his own admission of guilt.

"Carson said, 'I want you to run two detectives on the polygraph to see if they have perjured themselves. I have reason to believe they lied under oath.'

"I told the Sheriff, 'That's not the way we do it, Sheriff. The proper way is to run the suspect first to test his veracity, then if the polygraph examination indicates he did not make the oral confession, then we test the detectives.'

"Carson said, 'Well, however you do it, do it. I just want it done.'

"I had the suspect brought in and I attached the polygraph sensors. But before I could even start the examination, he ripped the leads off and said, 'What the fuck are you doing this for? I've confessed and been convicted. What's this all about? Take me back to jail.'

69

"I reported what happened to Sheriff Carson. He said, 'Well, you can go back to Tallahassee.' "

Ivie went on to relate what he had learned from debriefing his subordinate Joe Townsend about Townsend's recent assignment to Jacksonville. Agent Townsend said it was obvious to him that Sheriff Carson was attempting to falsely incriminate Cody and Coleman. Ivie then said, "You two better be careful. It's obvious Sheriff Carson's out to get you. I don't know why, and I don't want to know. I don't want to get involved with this. I just knew it was wrong, and my conscience demanded that I let you know. Good luck. "

The detectives never saw Ivie again. The detectives knew very well that Agent Ivie purposely remained longer than needed at the Sheriff's office that day so that he could warn the detectives about what had happened. If he had not, Cody and Coleman would have never known about Sheriff Carson's latest attempt to falsely incriminate them. Sergeants Cody and Coleman were extremely grateful for Agent Ivie's revelations. Agent Ivie had taken an enormous chance. If word ever got out about Ivie's warnings to the detectives, he would have surely lost his job. All it would have taken would have been one phone call to the director of the Florida Sheriff's Bureau from Sheriff Carson to kill that messenger. Suddenly, the purpose of Chief Patrick's presence in court the day of the rape trial became readily apparent. He was again conspiring with Sheriff Carson to find a way to frame Detectives Cody and Coleman. He may have just been sending them a signal—*I'm going to get you two whistle blowers, one way or another*.

Now get this picture in your mind about Sheriff Carson. He was a former FBI officer, a man who wore a big white hat in the eyes of Duval County citizens, an image created and perpetuated by Jacksonville's corrupt news media, both print and broadcast. His wife was a beautiful, prominent and highly respected gynecologist, and her clientele included many of the wives of the Duval County powerbrokers. The respect that Doctor Carson had earned from her patients, for the most part, enabled and increased Dale Carson's own influence and prestige in Duval County.

Sheriff Carson was perceived by the county's citizens to be a public official of honesty and integrity. While capable of great public charisma, the detectives knew Sheriff Carson also had a Machiavellian side. In addition, Sheriff Carson was often cold, aloof, and abrasive with the personnel under him. In fact, the detectives had a standing joke:

"I passed the Sheriff today and he spoke to me."

"What did he say?"

"Get out of the way, boy."

The only time Sheriff Carson even appeared in the detective division was at Christmas when he handed out baskets of fruit.

However, it was not Sheriff Carson's personality or fruit gifts that concerned the detectives at this point. Sheriff Carson was unpredictable and inscrutable. Unless another convicted felon fortuitously offered to provide information of another attempted frame, the detectives might not know what else Sheriff Carson and Chief Patrick had attempted in the past or would attempt in the future.

They would soon learn.

*   *   *

In May of 1964, a very active armed robber made the news. He was known to law enforcement as the Bubble Glass Bandit. Bubble Man had committed a string of armed robberies in Duval County, targeting people at various

71

businesses located in strip malls, and shopping centers. There was a BOLO (*Be on the lookout for*) outstanding for this criminal. He was always well dressed and wore very dark and rather large bulbous (bubble) sunglasses, which were fashionable at the time. He typically donned a snap-brim hat, tie and sport coat.

One afternoon, as Detectives Cody and Coleman drove by the Highlands Shopping Center located at the intersection of Soutle Drive and Moncrief Road, they observed a white male who resembled the description provided to them by police artists. They observed the suspect slowly pacing up and down in front of a Winn-Dixie Grocery.

"Coleman," Sergeant Cody said. "There's our suspect, the Bubble Glass Bandit. Let's go around the building so he won't see us and come up behind him."

The detectives' intuition had kicked in, and they felt the man intended to rob the Winn-Dixie Grocery, perhaps waiting for customers to thin down before he entered the store.

Detectives Cody and Coleman circled the businesses and entered a pharmacy next to Winn-Dixie through the back door. Identifying themselves as detectives to the pharmacy staff, they moved to the front of the store intending to exit and obtain a vantage point to observe the Bubble Man's actions. If they did not see him when they exited the pharmacy, they would assume that he had entered the Winn-Dixie to perpetrate a robbery. In that case, the detectives would position themselves outside the door to apprehend the robber as he attempted to flee.

Just as Detectives Cody and Coleman reached the front door of the pharmacy store to exit, the suspect appeared in front of the pharmacy. Bubble Man stopped and studied his own reflection in the pharmacy's glass window. Bubble Man took off his hat and bubble sunglasses, wiped his sunglasses and forehead with a handkerchief, and replaced the hat and dark sunglasses.

Sergeant Cody thought, *Buddy, whoever you are, I've seen you now.* Cody observed that the pharmacy lunch counter cash register was located immediately adjacent to the front door, so he thought the bandit might have targeted this store instead of the Winn-Dixie. Sergeant Cody pretended to study a postcard rack. A lunch counter customer left his seat, walked up to the register, and paid his bill. As the customer exited the store, "Bubble Man" turned and followed right behind him.

The customer, as subsequent investigation revealed, was a debit insurance salesman, who collected payments from his clients, usually door to door on Saturdays. On this particular Saturday, he had been collecting his debits all day, and was carrying a large amount of cash. It is possible that the bandit knew this somehow, perhaps by observing the salesman's route and schedule and had actually targeted the salesman specifically, rather than the pharmacy. The odds were against his choice of this victim being random. He may have even held a policy sold to him by this salesman.

Sergeant Cody immediately exited the store and fell in behind them both.

After the insurance man entered his vehicle and started the engine, and before the car began to move, "Bubble Man" inserted himself through the passenger-side window. Instantly, the driver's door swung open, and the intended victim rolled out onto the pavement shouting, "He's got a gun! He's got a gun and he's trying to rob me!"

At this point Sergeant Cody drew his .357 magnum from his shoulder holster and shouted, "Police officer. Don't move!"

The Bubble Glass Bandit ignored Sergeant Cody's command and dove completely into the victim's vehicle. Positioning himself in the driver's seat, Bubble Man threw the automatic gearshift into reverse, and backed up, with the driver's side window less than six feet from Cody and his magnum.

Sergeant Cody stepped closer cautiously, knowing the suspect must be armed. Detective Cody aimed his magnum through the open driver's side window at Bubble Man's ear and repeated his order to not move. Sergeant Cody really did not think the bandit would attempt to drive away. Instead of obeying Sergeant Cody's order, the bandit put the car in forward gear and accelerated toward the strip mall exit. Sergeant Cody discharged his magnum and blew the left rear tire out to thwart Bubble Man's escape. However, the loss of the tire did not stop the bandit. He pushed the gas pedal to the floor and drove on, a shower of sparks flying from the rim of the flat left rear wheel. The shower of sparks reminded Cody of a rooster tail created by a high speed racing hydroplane.

At this point, Sergeant Cody having witnessed an armed robbery and auto theft was duty-obligated to take any action necessary to stop the Bubble Man's escape. Detective Cody then fired three rounds of the magnum through the back window of the fleeing vehicle. The bandit was lucky. The bullets shattered the back window, narrowly missing the bandit, with the bullets passing by each side of his head. Bubble Man scrunched down as far as he could in the front seat and drove on, exiting the strip mall parking lot on three wheels. He turned onto Soutel Drive and headed east.

When the shooting started, several female shoppers started screaming, even though they were not in the line of fire. While Cody was firing at the fleeing armed robber in the stolen car, Sergeant Coleman managed to gather the hysterical female shoppers together and successfully calm them down. Cody would later tease Coleman unmercifully about this, asking Coleman if the women would have been safer behind him instead of in front of him. Coleman never laughed at this joke.

Coincidentally, within minutes, Sergeant Cody observed Chief of Detectives Patrick and Sheriff Carson enter the parking lot and park at a distance from the crime scene. Both administrators remained in their vehicle and at no time approached or spoke to the detectives. The detectives wondered if Chief Patrick and Sheriff Carson had been tailing them. If so, for how long? Had they followed them on other days as well?

Detectives Cody and Coleman returned to their vehicle, gave the dispatcher a description of the stolen vehicle, and requested assistance from any officers who might be in the area. Shortly, while Detectives Cody and Coleman were interviewing the robbery victim, a Duval County patrol motorcycle officer advised over the radio that he had located the stolen vehicle, sitting in the middle of the street in a residential neighborhood, just east of the strip mall. Ironically, the neighborhood was called Sherwood Forest; only in this case, no arrows were flying through the forest air this day, only the rounds of Sergeant Cody's .357 magnum.

The motorcycle officer was standing by the stolen vehicle when the detectives arrived. A neighbor came out of her house and said she had seen the driver exit the vehicle and she pointed out the house that the man had run into. By that time, several other patrol cars had arrived on the scene. The officers surrounded the house and ordered the man to exit. Bubble Man complied and was taken into custody.

Bubble Man's wife exited the dwelling with him. Her name was Betty Rafuse. She was a member of the Rafuse family, a well-known and brutal criminal family in Duval County. Sergeant Cody knew members of this family well. Otto Rafuse, Betty's father, was a legendary tush hog, a bar fighter and bootlegger with a long criminal record. Truman Rafuse, one of Betty's brothers, was serving a life sentence at that time in the Florida State Penitentiary for murder.

Russell Rafuse was another of Betty's brothers, who like the other family members, had a very extensive criminal record. In fact, Sergeant Cody, as a uniformed deputy, had previously arrested Russell for breaking and entering. One night, Sergeant Cody and his riding partner Earl Taylor were responding to a silent alarm drop and confronted Russell Rafuse and his criminal accomplice as the thieves were exiting the RCA warehouse, a rural distribution center on Ellis Road. In the resulting exchange of gunfire, Sergeant Cody was wounded. A round from a pistol struck the corner of the warehouse wall and splintered into Cody's right forearm. Russell managed to escape into the woods, but was captured later about a mile from the scene. Russell's accomplice was badly wounded in his left foot. He escaped also but was apprehended when he later sought medical treatment for his wound.

Sergeant Cody often thought about the Bubble Glass Bandit incident and how he and members of the Rafuse family seemed to be destined to cross paths.

The Bubble Glass Bandit was arrested and charged, but before he was tried, the detectives would see him again.

Sometime later, around September of 1964, a corrections officer (called jailers in those days) contacted Sergeant Cody and related the following: "We've got an inmate named James Bramlett [Bubble Man], and he has requested that we contact you and see if you and Sergeant Coleman could confer with him at the jail."

Sergeant Cody said, "Yes, we can talk with him. Please place him in a holding cell."

After the detectives arrived they escorted James Bramlett (the Bubble Man) to an interrogation room in the county jail. Bramlett's first statement to the detectives was, "What the fuck have you guys done? It looks to me like the Sheriff is out to get you two officers."

Again, Sergeant Cody asked, "James, what in the world makes you say that? What do you want to tell us? It's obvious after that statement that you know something we need to know."

Bramlett continued and said, "Almost immediately after I was locked up, I was transported to Chief Patrick's office in the courthouse. After I arrived, Chief Patrick said he was talking on behalf of Sheriff Dale Carson and offered me every deal in world--anything I wanted if I'd implicate you and Sergeant Coleman in a robbery with me. I refused. The only reason I'm telling you this, Sergeant Cody is because you had a pistol in my ear that day you arrested me, and you could have legally blown my brains out, but you didn't."

"You're right, James. I could have legally shot you, but I chose not to."

"You gave me a chance on that day and that's why I'm telling you now what Chief Patrick offered me. They are out to bury you. I think you guys had better watch yourselves. Please don't reveal that I contacted you. If Patrick finds out I talked to you about this, you know my ass would be grass."

The detectives thanked James Bramlett and left. As they were leaving the county jail, the detectives reflected on how the irony of how it seemed that convicted felons were protecting them. Who were the bad guys here?

Detectives Coleman and Cody later (about 1982) located James Bramlett who had taken up residence in New York. They asked Bramlett if he would be willing to testify on their behalf in their pending Civil Rights suit they had filed in federal court. Bramlett declined to testify. He said, "I hate to say no, but I've moved away from Jacksonville. Nobody knows me here or about my criminal background. I haven't been in trouble for years. Because I want to protect my family, I just can't get involved."

"Your testimony would be helpful, James," Sergeant Cody said.

Bramlett replied, "I already helped you once."

"I understand," Cody said. "Thanks again for what you did, James."

Both Detectives Cody and Coleman did understand the man's desire to start his life over, and the detectives knew that if the matter were pushed, the man might have a sudden lapse in memory anyway, or worse, say something that might even damage their case if he went was forced to testify against his will.

Yet, Sergeant Cody too wished that he could start his life over—he and the other detectives had lost so much of their lives fighting corruption in the Duval County Sheriff's Office. And via the Civil Rights case they had filed, Sergeant Cody and the other victims hoped to get some of that lost life back.

Chapter Nine:
Civil Servants

Fraud and falsehood only dread examination.
Truth invites it
                    .—Samuel Johnson

For Detectives Cody, Coleman, and West, 1964 was a tough year. However, trouble for the detectives continued to escalate. It was hard for them to believe that their conflict and difficulties with Sheriff Carson and Chief Patrick had begun with a simple Civil Service exam. It was the promotional exam for Detective Lieutenant, which has already been discussed to some degree, but because of the test's importance and complexity, the author feels it necessary to discuss it in greater detail.

In 1964, to be eligible to take a promotional exam, an officer was required to have a year's service in the previous rank. The difference between the income of a Detective Sergeant and Detective Lieutenant was significant enough to make it a desirable promotion. Once a detective became a lieutenant, he would become eligible for higher ranks and positions, such as captain and even ranks above captain such as Chief.

However, the detectives who took the test discovered that promotion and advancement would, one way or another, ultimately only be awarded to those loyal to Sheriff Carson and Chief of Detectives Patrick. A test that should have rewarded knowledge, skill, and the wisdom of hard-earned experience was used instead as a club and control mechanism to maintain the power of the corrupt, to assure the promotion of team players, and to keep dissidents in line.

The exam was given on a hot July 23, 1964. The test was composed of at least fifty questions, all multiple-choice. The test had been created by an outside agency that created Civil Service tests for agencies nationwide. There were eighteen applicants for the test.

The results were posted quickly. At this time, there were two vacancies for Detective Lieutenant. Civil Service law dictated that the two sergeants receiving the highest grades would be promoted to detective lieutenant. Testers received a certain number of points for seniority and twenty percent of the test grade depended upon the most recent progress report grade provided by their supervisor. Though as previously pointed out, the detectives did not know that progress reports had not been submitted by Chief Patrick for over two years, in direct violation of Civil Service law.

The two detectives with the highest scores on this occasion were Sergeant Claude West and Sergeant Donald Coleman. On the morning after the test was given and graded, as soon as Sergeants Cody and West entered the detective division, Annie Smith, a secretary assigned to the records division, called them over.

"Congratulations," Smith said. "I just talked to my aunt, Mrs. Dorsey, who you know is executive secretary of the Civil Service Board. Well, Aunt Louise just told me that you Sergeant West came in first and Sergeant Coleman second on the Lieutenant's exam."

That same morning, Lieutenant Ray Headen went to the Civil Service Board Office and viewed the posted test results. He removed the posted results and asked one of the office personnel to make a copy of the test results, so he could post them in the Detective Division.

Before the results could be copied, Civil Service Board Executive Secretary Louise Dorsey (Annie Smith's aunt) stopped the secretary from making the copy, took it from the secretary and declared, "There's been a mistake in the grading, and we're going to have to grade the tests again."

Lieutenant Headen left without any test results in his hand.

Because of her position as Executive Secretary, at that time Detective Headen chose to not question Louise Dorsey's actions. The detective waited expectantly the rest of the day, but no new test results were posted.

However, the next morning, Louise Dorsey appeared in the Detective Division with an armful of folders. The rest of the day and the next day, she and Chief Patrick were sequestered in Chief Patrick's office behind closed doors. The detectives who took the test were suspicious, but had no way of knowing what was going on and did not dare inquire. However, all the detectives were extremely apprehensive because of the long closed-door meetings.

On August 6, 1964, the Civil Service Board met in Executive Session and received the new compilation of final exam grades from Executive Secretary Louise Dorsey. When the new results were posted, the results indicated sergeants Roland Grant and Richard Fleming were promoted to the rank of Detective Lieutenant instead of Sergeants Claude West and Donald Coleman.

After some probing, the detectives discovered what had happened.

Evidently, Employee Progress Reports were not utilized in tabulating the original test scores. The reason: None existed. The Civil Service Board inquired of Board Attorney John Cox if the progress reports should have been considered in tabulating test scores, and he stated his opinion that the wording of the Civil Service law indicated the progress reports positively should have been included. The Civil Service Board, acting on his advice, ruled that the Employee Progress Reports should have been utilized and directed Sheriff Carson to provide the required progress reports.

Here is where a real problem arose for the detectives. Though the reports were indeed legally required, in actuality there had been no Employee Progress Report submitted to the Civil Service Board for over two years. Obviously, the Civil Service Board did not know of the neglected submission of the required progress reports when Louise Dorsey first tabulated and posted the test results. How is it possible for people who had worked with the Civil Service Board for many years to make such an important omission?

The failure to submit the employee progress reports has to be laid on Chief of Detectives J. C. Patrick, for it was his legal responsibility to submit these reports and his failure to do so was a direct violation of Civil Service law. As directed by the Civil Service Board, Chief Patrick produced progress reports for those taking the exam and then submitted them to Sheriff Carson for his signature.

Sheriff Carson, on July 30, signed off on Chief Patrick's belated progress reports and forwarded them to the Civil Service Board. However, it should be pointed out that the progress reports were *created* seven days after the promotional exam was given and graded. Civil Service law required that the most recent Employee Progress Report submitted *prior* to the promotional exam be utilized.

Nevertheless, the newly created and fraudulent reports found their way to the Civil Service Board.

Already blacklisted and out of favor with both Chief Patrick and Sheriff Carson, Detectives Donald Coleman and Claude West were given very low grades on Patrick's new (and fraudulent) progress reports. Obviously, any document that could affect the final grade of any already graded test by 20% would allow those responsible for final compilation of the test grades to promote whomever they chose. And with the promotion of Sergeants Roland Grant and Richard Fleming to Detective Lieutenant, that is exactly what happened.

Sergeant Coleman decided to bring the matter of this blatant fraud to the attention of Sheriff Carson. Though Cody did not take the test—he was a few months' away from eligibility—because of his close friendship and alliance with Coleman and other officers, he immersed himself right into the conflagration that the test ignited. Sergeant Cody chose to stand by Coleman's side in this and go to Sheriff Carson with him because it was glaringly apparent that criminal fraud had been committed, and Cody felt it was his duty to report the crime. Like so many of the "small" issues the detectives faced, the matters surrounding the promotional examination for Detective Lieutenant for the Duval County Sheriff's Office should have been easy to address and correct.

It should have been, but it wasn't.

Sergeants Cody and Coleman met with Sheriff Carson and informed him of the obviously fraudulent action and conspiracy of Chief Patrick and Executive Secretary Louise Dorsey and of the progress report forms created seven days after the exam was given and graded. Sergeant Cody said, "The reason we're here, Sheriff, is because your signature is affixed to those fraudulent documents. We know you are a busy man and did not realize what was going on when you signed them. And we are sure that Chief Patrick and Louise Dorsey didn't tell you. We also knew you would not want in any way to be part of this criminal conduct." Sergeant Cody showed Sheriff Carson a copy of the forged progress report that bore his signature, dated July 30, 1964.

Sheriff Carson seemed shocked and appalled. Sheriff Carson then said, "Oh, my God. I had no knowledge of this. I should have paid more attention to what was going on. I cannot thank you enough for bringing this to my attention. I will immediately bring this criminal conduct to the attention of State Attorney Hallowes. " Sheriff Carson strongly affirmed that he would not allow the new and fraudulent exam results to stand.

Though the detectives thought they had efficiently handled the issue by appealing to Sheriff Carson, actually they had only played into Chief Patrick's hands. They were not happy when they learned on August 19 that Sheriff Carson had knowingly, and in direct violation of the law, certified the illegal promotions of Roland Grant and Richard Fleming from Detective Sergeant to Detective Lieutenant.

With the exception of the illegally appointed and promoted Sergeants Grant and Fleming, on August 25, 1964 several of the detective sergeants who had taken the Lieutenant's Promotional Exam on July 23, 1964, retained legal counsel and contested the results. Rather than attack the issue of the progress reports, which was a battle their lawyer felt they could not win, their lawyer advised them to attack the test itself and contend that a multitude of the questions and answers on the test were ambiguous or incorrect. Subsequently, an arbitrator was assigned to determine the validity of their legal contentions.

On November 19, 1964, the Civil Service Board met again in Executive Session and announced that after a review of the Lieutenant Detective Exam, the assigned arbitrator found that thirteen of the test questions used were ambiguous or misleading and erroneous. After the arbitrator's determination, the Civil Service Board met in executive session on November 19, 1964. The board expressed their agreement with the arbitrator announced that after review of the flawed detective lieutenant exam, that thirteen of the questions of the detective lieutenant exam were flawed. The board therefore revoked the test results and revoked the promotions that Sheriff Carson had certified and considered the appointments made by such certification vitiated and annulled. The board also decided that a new exam for Detective Lieutenant would be created and a new test date announced at the earliest, most practical date.

The new test date for promotion to Detective Lieutenant was set for January 8, 1965. However, Circuit Judge Marion Gooding issued an injunction on behalf of Detectives Roland Grant and Richard Fleming that blocked the new test and the new test date, so the Civil Service Board cancelled the scheduled test.

The difficulties Sheriff Carson encountered in this situation spurred his creative thinking and he took steps to make sure he would not encounter resistance again.

After the Civil Service Board cancelled the test, Chairman Carl Taylor, whom the detectives knew to always side with what was right, contacted Sergeant Claude West. Taylor said, "I've tried to contact Representative Lynwood Arnold [the chairman of the Duval delegation] by phone at the capital and can't reach him. I've got to get a message to him. I've just learned that Sheriff Carson is going to Tallahassee tomorrow in an attempt to alter the Civil Service law, giving him the latitude to make personnel transfers interdepartmentally." Chairman Taylor went on to explain the implications of this intended change.

This was an obvious effort on Carson's part to circumvent the oversight of the Civil Service Board. Practically, it meant he could arbitrarily transfer men from one department to another as he wished. For example, a jailer might be transferred to the detective division, or a detective could be transferred to the uniform division. Regardless of seniority, after each transfer the employee would have to go through a six-month probationary period, such as what they were subject to when they were first hired. This would give Sheriff Carson the power to easily and quickly terminate any employee he desired to remove from the Sheriff's Office for incompetence, insubordination, etc.

Chairman Taylor continued. "I've also been advised that Sheriff Carson intends to tell the legislative delegation that his requested new transfer policy has the full endorsement and blessing of the Civil Service Board. This is not true." Taylor requested Sergeant West to take his attorney to Tallahassee the next day, about a two and a half hour drive, and advise the Duval Delegation head, Representative Lynwood Arnold, that if Sheriff Carson made that assertion, that it was an unequivocal lie. Taylor said, "Mr. Arnold can call me if he wants and I'll verify the fact that the board has not endorsed Sheriff Carson's proposed alteration of the Civil Service law."

Sergeant Cody is puzzled even today as to why Taylor did not pursue the matter himself. Taylor was advanced in age. Perhaps he wanted to help but did not want to attract attention to himself. In addition, to make an official statement of the board, he would have had to gather all the members together in session, and there just was not time enough to do that.

Claude West did rise early and make the drive to Tallahassee with his attorney, Thomas McKee, who was representing the deputies in the Civil Service test challenge.

When they entered the legislative chambers, Sergeant West and Attorney McKee were confronted by Sheriff Carson. Carson asked, "What are you two doing here?"

West responded, "We're here at the request of Civil Service Board Chairman Carl Taylor who said you were going to lie to the legislature."

When they found Representative Arnold, they communicated to him the information supplied by Chairman Taylor. Arnold replied that Sheriff Carson had already testified that his requested Civil Service rules change had the blessing of the Duval County Civil Service Board. Representative Arnold then called Chairman Taylor and confirmed the fact that Sheriff Carson's rule change did not have the blessing of the board. Later that day in open legislative session, Arnold admonished Sheriff Carson for making false statements. Arnold said, "I've just spoken to Chairman Taylor of the Duval County Civil Service Board and he emphatically denies that you have their blessing or permission for your proposed changes." The Florida Legislature then denied Sheriff Carson's request. Had the Duval delegation properly reported this violation to the governor as required by their oath of office, Carson would have lost his job. However, Carson escaped damage, suffering only the minor humiliation and sting of Representative Arnold's rebuke.

Sheriff Carson was not happy with this setback, but Dale Carson was a very determined and politically powerful man, and he knew how to use people and position to get what he wanted. And now, more than ever, Sheriff Carson wanted to get rid of the troublesome and crusading detectives.

Chapter Ten:
Reassignment

"You wore out your welcome mat . . . I never liked you anyhow. . .You're in the doghouse now"
—from a song by Brenda Lee.

Late in 1964, Sheriff Carson determined that Detectives Cody and Coleman were a liability and loose cannons in their present position, capable of destroying Sheriff Carson's carefully crafted image of honesty and integrity. Carson's image had been shaped by years of support from the corrupt Jacksonville media—both print and broadcast, especially the *Florida Time Union*, Jacksonville's prominent newspaper. So, the sheriff decided to divide and conquer. Both were reassigned.

Originally, the Sheriff's Office policy required all detectives in the detective teams to serve criminal warrants on an alternating basis. The criminal warrant workload was so overwhelming that the department had two permanent warrant details.

There were plenty of warrants, stacks of them. They did not have to look around for any work. Sergeant Coleman was assigned to one warrant detail and Sergeant Cody to another. This new assignment required the detectives to serve felony criminal warrants to the most dangerous criminals. This was the most dangerous assignment in the department. Such men and women were not always eager to go to prison.

They also served competency warrants. If the doctors examined a suspect felt he was mentally incompetent or a danger to himself or others, the evidence was presented to the county judge and if the evidence warranted action, the judge would issue an *incompetency* warrant. In many cases, when the detectives attempt to execute service of such warrants, the recipients had to be restrained by physical force.

At that point, Sergeant Cody was not very thrilled with his new warrant detail assignment. Detective Cody's new riding partner was Deputy Robert Stringer, a retired Navy chief, who incidentally was an international pistol champion in the Navy. Well educated and humorous, he related to Cody the events surrounding the service of an incompetency warrant on a female. As his partner was sick on that day, he was required to serve the warrant alone. The woman was not cooperative and she somehow got the drop on him with a double barrel shotgun and relieved Stringer of his .44 magnum revolver, the car keys, and the warrant. The woman then said, "Okay, Deputy Dawg, walk into the sunset and leave your horse here."

With the setting sun in his eyes, Detective Stringer departed the scene on foot and called for assistance when he reached the nearest phone. Sheriff Office personnel who heard the dispatcher responding to Stringer's telephone call began to refer to the woman immediately as the new Sheriff of Riverview. Later, Stringer found out that the woman was well known to the Sheriff's Office and there had been previous "dehorsing" incidents. Officers returned to the woman's home, retrieved Stringer's "horse" and .44 magnum, taking the Sheriff of Riverview into custody.

Sergeant Cody thanked Deputy Stringer for warning him of the perils of the warrant detail.

Around November of 1964, Sergeant Cody was reassigned to normal detective duty and paired with Sgt. John Britts. Coleman remained assigned to the warrant detail. The vacancy to where Cody was moved likely came up due to a retirement, and they needed someone to fill that spot. Chief Patrick and Sheriff Carson had actually accomplished their purpose by separating Cody and Coleman.

While Cody and Coleman were serving warrants, it is important to know what was taking place in the background, events that gave them hope, but like previous glimmers of hope, events that would prove disappointing in the end.

Chapter Eleven:
Trial by Denial

Good lawyers know the law;
great lawyers know the judge.
— Author Unknown

James A. Davis was the only tush hog murderer of Johnnie Mae Chappell not in custody. Therefore, a fugitive warrant was issued and two Duval County detectives were dispatched to arrest him at Ft. Bragg, N.C. Davis' trial date was set for November 30, 1964. Upon his return to Jacksonville, he was placed in solitary confinement for approximately thirty days. During his confinement, not one member of the Sheriff's Office, State Attorney's Office, or FBI ever contacted him. Davis' attorney informed him that he was not going to be tried and he could go home. And that is just what he did. Obviously, it appeared the state did not intend to try him in the first place.

The only tush hog to be tried was J.W. Rich, the shooter. As an example of American justice, that trial was less than stellar. State Attorney William A. Hallowes, obviously working in concert with defense counsel, carried out the crime of obstruction of justice in a textbook fashion. In legal terms, Hallowes perpetrated acts of malfeasance, misfeasance, and nonfeasance. Consider the following:

1. Of the myriad of witnesses subpoenaed to testify, only Detective Sergeant Donald R. Coleman was called.

2. When Sergeants Cody and Coleman, responded to their *subpoena ducas tecum* [bring the evidence], they were informed by the property room custodian that the Chappell .22 caliber murder weapon that they had properly tagged, bagged and booked into evidence was missing from the property room. Mr. Howard, the property room custodian, could not explain the disappearance of the evidence. According to Custodian Howard, property room records indicated the murder weapon was still booked and had never been removed. Having been removed from the case by Chief J.C. Patrick, Detectives Cody and Coleman had no way of knowing if any additional ballistic evidence had been recovered, booked, marked and placed into evidence. Such ballistic evidence would have included the actual projectile—if one had been recovered from Chappell's body. Additional ballistic tests should have been made attempting to match the recovered bullet to the recovered murder weapon, and those records should have been inserted into the Chappell investigative file. When the detectives queried Mr. Howard further as to whether any such ballistic evidence had been submitted to the property room and was now missing, he responded that no ballistic evidence other than the revolver related to the Chappell homicide had been submitted to him.

Extremely disturbed by this information, Detectives Cody and Coleman immediately proceeded to the office of State Attorney Hallowes and met with First Assistant State Attorney Nathan Shavitz. The detectives informed Shavitz of the missing murder weapon. Shavitz responded by saying, "Go have a seat in the witness chambers and don't worry about it."

Sergeants Cody and Coleman knew that something was terribly amiss. They knew that for Rich to be successfully prosecuted for premeditated first-degree murder as charged by the grand jury indictment, the firearm used by the shooter would have to be in the state's possession.

Later, Sergeants Cody and Coleman's apprehensions were proven to be well founded. They learned that the .22 revolver the detectives had recovered was never submitted as evidence in the trial by the state. A projectile had been recovered from the victim's body the day after her murder. Detective Cody possesses an official copy of a release signed by Lieutenant Roland Grant that indicates that on March 24, 1964, the morning after Mrs. Chappell had been murdered, Grant had received the bullet from the medical examiner's office, but Grant had never properly booked this crucial evidence in the evidence locker. Detectives Cody and Coleman had suspicions that the bullet had been stored in the desk of Chief J. C. Patrick, the original obstructer of justice in the Chappell homicide.

The detectives were appalled to later learn how the state conducted the trail of shooter, J.W. Rich. Official records show that State Attorney Hallowes presented a spent .22 projectile in a plain, unmarked and unsealed white manila envelope instead of a sealed, signed, evidence bag. Hallowes, with decades of prosecutorial experience, knew this projectile had no evidentiary value when handled and introduced to the court in this fashion, particularly since he presented no supporting ballistic evidence, to wit, the recovered murder weapon needed to be ballistically tied to the submitted projectile recovered in the Chappell homicide. State Attorney Hallowes knew that all the defense counsel would have to say to challenge this improperly submitted forensic evidence was, "What is that? Where did it come from? Obviously, it was not properly booked into evidence. What's that projectile got to do with my client?"

Hallowes would have replied, "Well, that's the bullet that killed Mrs. Chappell and your client is the one that shot her."

The defense counsel would have immediately retorted, "My client shot her with what? Where is the murder weapon? Where are the ballistic tests to tie that bullet to a weapon and a weapon to my client? Why is this bullet not properly marked as evidence? This evidence is tainted and of no evidentiary value. Your honor, I move for a mistrial."

Any judge with trial experience would have surely granted that motion. It would be fair to say that for the State Prosecutor to handle and introduce evidence in this manner it would be absolutely contrary to the well-established, rudimentary, investigative procedure required to preserve the most critical chain of forensic evidence. Hallowes' flawed presentation of critical forensic evidence in this fashion would surely have negated any chance of a successful prosecution.

Yet, none of this dialogue took place. Judge, prosecutor, and defense counsel allowed this abrogation of jurisprudence in the trial of J.W. Rich to continue as planned.

Susan Armstrong, in her article, "Murder on New Kings Road," published in the Jacksonville *Folio Weekly* on January 01, 2001, says this about the results of the trial:

State Attorney William Hallowes [more correctly the grand jury] charged Rich with first-degree murder, but after two days of testimony, an all white male jury found Rich guilty of the lesser included offense of manslaughter. He was sentenced to 10 years in prison. All charges were dropped against the remaining three, and they were released. (21)

The official court docket entry made by the State Prosecutor's office on January 18, 1965, states this:

Wayne M. Chessman and James Alex Davis appeared in open court with counsel. Wayne E. Ripley appeared for defendant Elmer L. Kato. Assistant State Attorney Nathan Schavitz moved for entry of *nolle prosequi* as to each defendant, stating that the evidence was insufficient for trial. Judge John McNatt granted the motion and each defendant was discharged and his bond cancelled.

This official court docket entry is in direct conflict with the investigative facts contained in the *corpus delecti* of the Chappell homicide. The claim by state prosecutors that the state's evidence was insufficient for trial is an absolute, blatant, and premeditated lie.

Chapter Twelve:
Meeting Governor Haydon Burns

*As the governor of this state, I obviously
see the issue quite differently.*
– Gray Davis, Governor of California

Before he became the thirty-fifth governor of Florida, Haydon Burns was Mayor and Police Commissioner of the city of Jacksonville. He served four terms as mayor and his efforts to promote Jacksonville gained the city international recognition. He was extremely popular among Jacksonville's citizens.

Yet, in spite of his popularity, Burns also had significant enemies. Like most other Jacksonville officials, he had opposed consolidation, the movement that basically desired to turn the whole of Duval County into the City of Jacksonville. If implemented, consolidation would have immediately obliterated every elected office in the city. In other words, the current elected officials, including the city commissioners, would be out of work, unless of course they were fortunate enough to obtain a post in the new government.

Sheriff Carson and Chief Patrick in the Duval County Sheriff's Office would definitely be counted as enemies of Burns. The demonic duo—Sheriff Carson and Chief Patrick—had no desire to see Burns become governor, so they set out on a campaign to discredit him.

Like Sheriff Carson and Chief Patrick, Burns also had a dark side, but he concealed it well. His nickname was

"Old Slick." Burns knew which way the wind was blowing in America on the issue of race and did a fairly good job at pleasing both sides of the race issue. For example, Burns appointed the first black policeman in Jacksonville in 1950. The police department ended up with several black officers, but these officers were only allowed to work in the black areas of town and could not arrest whites.

The city of Jacksonville also seemed to be more "people friendly" than the County. For example, Donald Coleman once asked Sheriff Carson to donate blood from the Sheriff Office's blood bank for his dying daughter, Donna, who had a chronic condition known as portal hypertension. Sheriff Carson refused to furnish Sergeant Coleman's dying daughter the blood she desperately needed. Sergeant Coleman then took his request to Chief Tiny Branch at the City of Jacksonville Police Department. Chief Branch told Sergeant Coleman that the City of Jacksonville would provide all the blood he needed from their blood bank to help his daughter. However, sadly, Donna Coleman succumbed to the disease and died not long after.

Like Sheriff Carson, Burns had his loyal soldiers. One was Tiny Branch, the Chief of Police in Jacksonville. Tiny's brother George was in charge of the black police precinct.

One veteran Jacksonville female police officer, a cousin of Sergeant Cody's and now deceased, related to Cody during one of her "beer-a-thons" that during her tenure as a Jacksonville police officer she served as a bag lady for Mayor Haydon Burns. She was required to be at Burns' office every Monday at 8:00 a.m. with her collections bag. Her superior who assigned her this task said that she better not be late—ever.

Haydon Burns gubernatorial campaign was successful and he was elected Governor of the State of Florida on January 5, 1965.

Shortly after Burns' election, on January 11, 1965, an article appeared in the *Florida Times Union* stating that two Duval County Road Patrol Officers had resigned from the Sheriff's Office to seek better employment. Rumors circulated within the county and city law enforcement communities that the two Duval County officers, Claude Bryant and Woodrow Pruitt had not resigned to seek better employment but had in fact committed the crimes of burglary and grand larceny.

During that time frame, Roy Sands appeared at the Sheriff's Office. Sands was a recently retired Duval County Detective Lieutenant who was now employed as a Deputy Constable under his brother, Constable Harry Sands. As a Sheriff's Office veteran, Roy Sands knew which detectives he could safely talk to. He spoke with several deputies telling them that Governor Burns had heard rumors that the recently resigned Road Patrol Officers, Pruitt and Bryant, had not actually resigned to seek better employment but committed a burglary and were apprehended by their superiors and not arrested. To conceal their crime from public scrutiny, both officers were allowed to resign and walk away scot-free. Deputy Constable Sands went on to say, "If any of you detectives have or can develop evidence that would verify these officers were in fact burglars, Governor Burns is extremely eager to receive that information. If any evidence is developed, contact me or my brother Constable Harry Sands."

Shortly after Deputy Constable Sands made contact with the Duval County detectives, Sergeant Cody and his new riding partner Sergeant John Britts were summoned to the home of the recently and illegally appointed Lieutenant Richard Fleming. Upon arrival at Fleming's home, Fleming

101

came outside and sat in the backseat of the detectives' cruiser. Fleming began the conversation by asking Cody and Britts if they knew _____, a new officer. Neither Cody nor Britts recognized the name.

Lieutenant Fleming said, "He came to see me last night. So you'll understand, I'm a long-time friend of his family and was a character reference for him when he applied for employment as a Duval County Road Patrol Officer. He related to me how he and three other officers were recently involved in the burglary of the Kenco Chemical Warehouse on Lem Turner Road. The senior officers, Woodrow Pruitt and Claude Bryant were forced to resign. He and the other rookie involved were allowed to keep their jobs, but were told to keep their mouths shut. 'The more you stir it, the more it stinks,' they were told. I told him that he had done the right thing and that if he wanted to keep his job and not go to jail to keep his mouth shut. I also told him that whatever he did to not cross Sheriff Carson or he would be very sorry."

To this day, Sergeant Cody is not sure why Lieutenant Fleming shared this news. Was it a sign of some kind of personal guilt? Was it a desire to protect the rookie friend? Was the knowledge of the cover-up just something he did not want to hold inside? Neither Sergeant Cody nor Sergeant Britts knew for sure.

Armed with this information, Sergeants Cody and Britts went directly to Constable Harry Sands and shared the newly acquired details.

The next day, Detective Sergeants—Lee Cody, Donald Coleman, John Britts, Claude West, Walter Becham, Hal Hanson, and William Mosley—were ordered by Governor Burns to meet him on the night of January 31, 1965, at 8:00 p.m. at his personal residence on Lorimar Road in Jacksonville. They were told again that the governor was interested in their firsthand personal knowledge of any criminal activity within the ranks of the Duval County Sheriff's Office. They were to bring this evidence in documented affidavit form. Thomas McKee, the attorney mentioned previously, was also ordered to attend.

At the ordered meeting Governor Burns was supplied the requested affidavits that addressed the crimes of criminal obstruction of justice committed by Sheriff Dale Carson and Chief of Detectives J.C. Patrick as well as the details related to the Civil Service Test fraud that had taken place in the promotional exams. Detectives Cody and Britts attested to the conversation they had had with Lieutenant Richard Fleming and what Fleming had revealed regarding the cover-up of the criminal activity of the uniformed officers who had burglarized the Kenco warehouse. The other detectives present presented numerous affidavits of burglaries and other criminal acts that involved Duval County Sheriff Office personnel.

Governor Burns was also furnished affidavits detailing acts of malfeasance, misfeasance, and nonfeasance committed by Fourth Judicial State Attorney William A. Hallowes, III. Cody and the others present pointed out that if, as Florida law and the state's constitution say, "A state attorney in Florida is not merely a prosecuting officer in the circuit in which he is elected, he is also an officer of the criminal law," then Hallowes failed miserably to fulfill the duties of his office.

After Governor Burns read each and every affidavit presented to him, he said, "I am ordering you, Constable Sands, to investigate all the criminal acts contained in the presented affidavits, and I'm ordering all of you officers present to assist Constable Sands in any matter he deems necessary and to follow his investigative instructions."

At that point, the governor thanked the detectives for coming and dismissed them. They were now special investigators for the governor. Constable Sands instructed the detectives to be at his office at 6:00 a.m. the following morning.

Upon arrival of the detectives at his office on Liberty Street the next morning, Constable Sands informed the new special investigators that he had decided that the first case to be investigated would be the burglary of the Kenco Chemical Company warehouse, as that crime had been the most recently reported. He then instructed that the two rookie officers involved be taken into custody and brought to his office. This was accomplished immediately.

Upon their arrival to his office, Constable Sands advised both of the rookie officers that he was acting on the direct orders of Governor Haydon Burns and that he had received information that they had been involved in the breaking and entering of the Kenco Chemical Company, located at the intersection of Lem Turner and Leonid roads. They were asked to submit sworn court-reported statements regarding the events surrounding that burglary. Constable Sands told them that court reporters were on the premises and standing by ready to record their sworn confessions.

Here is a summary of what was contained in the confessions of the two rookie officers. The first rookie to be deposed was the riding partner of Claude Bryant. He attested to the following:

On January 9, 1965, after acquiring a crowbar from Officer Claude Bryant's residence, they proceeded to the Kenco Chemical Company warehouse. Just as Officer Bryant had pried the locks from the doors, Officer Woodrow Pruitt and his rookie riding- partner arrived at the scene. Pruitt, Bryant, and Bryant's rookie riding partner removed what they wanted from the warehouse and placed it in their patrol cars. Some of this stolen merchandise was deposited on the property of Claude Bryant, who did not live too far from the crime scene. The rest of the loot was transported by Pruitt and his rookie partner to the Duval County Courthouse. At the Duval County Courthouse parking area Pruitt and the rookie began loading the stolen merchandise into Pruitt's personal car. At that point, their superiors, Captain William Hartley and Captain Elwin Danson, confronted them. They were ordered to place the stolen merchandise in the property room and to wait in the Duval Road Patrol assembly room.

After Officer Bryant arrived at the courthouse and parked his patrol car. He immediately departed in his own personal vehicle. However, Officer Bryant's rookie partner was seen by Captain Hartley and before he could leave the Road Patrol headquarters was directed to join Pruitt and the other rookie in the assembly room.

Captain Danson then summoned Lieutenant Maynard Crouse, the immediate supervisor of the officers involved in the burglary. Crouse was directed to type letters of resignation for Officers Pruitt and Bryant. Officer Pruitt, because he was present, was directed to immediately sign his letter of resignation, which stated he was resigning to seek better employment. Officer Bryant, who had already departed, returned later in the day and signed his resignation. The two rookies were brought into the office and ordered to submit written statements outlining and disclosing the details of the Kenco Chemical warehouse burglary. They were directed to not discuss the details of the burglary with anyone.

Constable Sands then directed that Lieutenant Crouse be taken into custody and brought to his office. Upon the lieutenant's arrival, Sands advised Lieutenant Crouse that the two rookie officers had already submitted sworn confessions regarding the burglary of the Kenco

Company Warehouse. Sands requested Crouse to offer a court-reported sworn statement regarding his own knowledge of that burglary, the resignation of officers Pruitt and Bryant and the involvement of the two rookie officers.

Lieutenant Crouse cooperated and submitted a statement in complete detail, specifically revealing how he had been ordered by his superior, Captain Elwin Danson, to type the reason for Pruitt's and Bryant's resignations to be "seeking better employment." He admitted to also typing the statements of the two rookie officers.

Lieutenant Crouse also informed Constable Sands that Chief William F. Johnston, the County Road Patrol Chief, was also present, fully informed and in accord with the content of the statements.

When the interviews were completed, Constable Sands contacted Governor Burns in Tallahassee and informed him of the cover-up, the content of the confessions of the two rookie patrolmen as well as the statement of Lieutenant Crouse. Governor Burns then directed Constable Sands to bring the official transcriptions to Tallahassee immediately. Constable Sands left that same day to take the completed transcripts to the Governor's Mansion.

After Governor Burns read the court reported statements and confessions provided by Constable Sands, Burns was outraged. However, it is important to note that Governor Burns' intense interest in the Kenco burglary was more than just a reflection of his desire to rid the state of Florida of crime and corruption. This was a personal matter.

Approximately six months before the gubernatorial election, officers of the Duval County Sheriff's Office, working in concert with the Jacksonville office of the

Federal Bureau of Investigation, conducted an investigation that resulted in the indictment and arrest of five high-ranking Jacksonville police officers for allegedly accepting bribes from a black gambler named Hodges McGee. As it turned out, all but one of the officers was acquitted. Only one uniformed officer spent any time in jail.

Burns was positive that this investigation had been launched to embarrass him and hinder his election to the governor's office. The reason Sheriff Carson and others so opposed Burns was because he had been such a successful opponent on the issue of Jacksonville consolidation. In fact, the issue of consolidation had been brought before the electorate on four separate occasions and had been solidly defeated. The last person that advocates of consolidation wanted as governor was Haydon Burns.

Burns also realized that at the exact same time that the Jacksonville officers under his command were investigated and indicted, that the Jacksonville Sheriff's Office had concealed felony criminal activity committed by officers under Sheriff Carson's command. The knowledge of this was more than Governor Burns could tolerate.

Upon Constable Sand's return to Jacksonville, the newly appointed special investigators were again summoned to his office. Sands gave an account of his trip. Cody said that Governor Burns seated himself, read each of the confessions from cover to cover, and then exclaimed, "I've got the son-of-a-bitch now!"

Chapter Thirteen:
The Magic Show - How Governor Burns and Sheriff Carson Changed Confessed Criminals into Undercover Operatives

It is almost always the cover-up
rather than the event that causes trouble
--Howard Baker

Once the detectives had been assured that Governor Burns would take appropriate action against Sheriff Carson, they once again felt vindicated and were certain that justice had taken off its blindfold and the corruption of Sheriff Carson, Chief Patrick, State Attorney Hallowes and others would be appropriately dealt with by the high standards of the laws of the state of Florida and the government of the United States.

Once again, they would be disappointed.

As expected, Governor Burns ordered Sheriff Carson to Tallahassee. Sheriff Carson arrived, accompanied by Duval County Road Patrol Chief W.F. Johnston and his subordinates, Captains Elwin Danson and William Hartley. News of Sheriff Carson's awkward position quickly spread through Duval County.

After Sheriff Carson returned to Jacksonville, with the usual assistance from the corrupt Jacksonville news media—both print and broadcast—his propaganda machine immediately went to work. Sheriff Carson issued a public statement to *his* media saying that the governor did not fully understand the events surrounding the Kenco Chemical warehouse burglary. Sheriff Carson claimed that the two young officers who confessed to Governor Burns investigators were in fact undercover agents who had been investigating the conduct of senior officers Woodrow Pruitt and Claude Bryant.

This declaration by Sheriff Carson is in direct and total conflict with the content of the sworn, court-reported confessions submitted by the two rookie officers and by their immediate supervisor Lieutenant Maynard Crouse to the governor's investigators. For example, one of the young officers swore in his confession that he had laid his head on the seat of the patrol car while the burglary was in progress. He attested that he did not see what happened at the crime scene and further, that he did not want to know or see. He said he knew that if he saw anything, he would be criminally involved and that "worried the hell out of him."

It would be fair to say that the language of this rookie's confession hardly sounds like that of an officer working undercover. If this rookie had been an undercover agent as claimed by Sheriff Carson, all he would have had to declare was, "You do not understand, Constable Sands. We were working undercover for the sheriff. Please call him for verification." Neither of the two rookies made that assertion during their four-hour long interrogation.

That the rookies were not undercover operatives is also obvious from the fact that no action was immediately taken against the two senior officers, even after the rookies submitted their signed and sworn statements, statements that were recorded by Lieutenant Crouse. The rookies would have obviously completed their assignment—they were eyewitnesses, part of the stolen merchandise had been recovered and marked for evidence, so why were not senior officers Officer Pruitt and Officer Bryant arrested immediately?

State Attorney William A. Hallowes, III again obstructed justice by supporting Sheriff Carson's false assertions by misinformation and propaganda he supplied to the *Jacksonville Journal, The Florida Times Union* and the broadcast media. Upon Sheriff Carson's return to Jacksonville, huge front-page headlines declared: "Hallowes Confirms Probe." Bill Sweisgood, a staff writer, wrote the article. In the article, State Attorney Hallowes claimed that Sheriff Carson had made him aware last week of an on-going undercover operation to monitor the activities of Duval County Road Patrol officers, Woodrow Pruitt and Claude Bryant. The article said, "[Sheriff Carson's] statement that an investigation has been under way into alleged violations by members of the Sheriff's Office was confirmed today . . . ."

This was a blatant lie, an undeniable act of malfeasance. State Attorney Hallowes knew very well that there was no ongoing investigation and no need for one.

To summarize the gist and effects of the Carson propaganda blitzkrieg, it was now apparent to Detective Cody and the other officers involved that Governor Burns had no plans to suspend or remove Sheriff Carson. In a press statement, Governor Burns said that he intended to give Sheriff Carson "time to act upon the matters with which he was confronted."

The translation of "time to act upon" would soon be seen to mean, "Get your magic show together."

It should be pointed out that the State Attorney Hallowes interviewed by Sweissgood was the same state attorney who with impunity committed malfeasance, misfeasance, and nonfeasance in the Johnnie Mae Chappell homicide and had allowed three of the grand-jury indicted perpetrators in that hate crime murder to go free and the shooter to be convicted of the lesser included offense of manslaughter instead of premeditated first degree murder. State Attorney Hallowes had also covered up Sheriff Carson and Chief Patrick's criminal obstruction of justice that permeated the Chappell homicide investigation.

In response to the furor surrounding Sheriff Carson and on the same day that the "Hallowes Confirms Probe" headlines appeared, the Jacksonville Ministerial Alliance ran an article in the *Jacksonville Journal* entitled, "Pastors Support Carson." The article quotes a letter from the Jacksonville Ministerial Alliance. In this letter, Reverend George C. Stuart, chairman of the Alliance stated:

Sheriff Dale Carson has the confidence of those citizens in our county who are resolved that the future of Jacksonville and Duval County shall be maintained in the highest public interest and respect . . . Sheriff Carson is a model for law enforcement officers throughout the nation. The pastors of Duval County do not intend to stand aside and allow the reputation and effectiveness of Sheriff Dale Carson to be either misused or abused. His future is too important to the future of Duval County.

Yet, some in Jacksonville did recognize the deceptive ploy of Sheriff Carson's propaganda machine. On February 2, only one day before Sweisgood's article, Lloyd Brown, another well-known police reporter for the *Jacksonville Journal*, wrote a feisty article in obvious conflict with Hallowe's confirmation statement by revealing that he had personally interviewed Sheriff Carson and asked the sheriff if Woodrow Pruitt and Claude Bryant had in fact committed the crimes of burglary, breaking and entering and grand larceny, and instead of being arrested they were allowed to tender false resignations. Brown said that Sheriff Carson emphatically replied that he *had* conducted an internal investigation, that those allegations were false, and that he had found *no evidence of a crime*.

Someone was lying.

The newly appointed investigators for the governor —including Cody, Coleman, West, and Headen—watched these unfolding events with dismay as it became painfully apparent that Governor Burns, instead of removing Sheriff Carson from office, as he was obligated under oath to do, intended to cover up Sheriff Carson's criminal activity.

Governor Burns had made an obvious deal with Sheriff Carson. Shortly after Sheriff Carson's call to Tallahassee, William A. Hallowes III dropped all charges against the high-ranking Jacksonville Police Department officers, but to maintain some appearance of legitimacy, one uniformed officer drew the short straw and was prosecuted in that case, ultimately serving minimal jail time.

In addition, apparently as another condition of the deal, Governor Burns decided that Chief of Detectives J. C. Patrick had to be dealt with. There had been bad blood between Burns and Patrick for some time. It seems that though Governor Burns was willing to work with and compromise with Sheriff Carson, he was not willing to extend the same goodwill to Sheriff Carson's Chief of Detectives, who had constantly and publicly bad-mouthed Burns in an effort to discredit him and impede his ability to become governor. In addition, Chief Patrick, working in concert with the Jacksonville Office of the FBI, had spearheaded the investigation that resulted in the indictment of the previously noted high-ranking Jacksonville City Police Department detectives. Chief Patrick's malice toward Mayor Burns was so great that at one point during the campaign against the Jacksonville Police Department, Chief Patrick said publicly, "I've got the slick-headed bastard now."

The meeked Sheriff Carson came into line with Governor Burns' edict. Not long after his return from Tallahassee, Chief of Detectives J.C. Patrick applied for a thirty-day sick-leave absence. When that sick leave was exhausted, he applied for and was granted another thirty days sick leave. He then requested a thirty-day leave of absence and that too was granted. During Patrick's ninety-day leave, Sheriff Carson was actively working his good-ole-boy network to find J.C. Patrick new employment.

Sheriff Carson succeeded in his endeavor, and J.C. Patrick resigned from the Sheriff's Office on June 15 of 1965. In a letter addressed to Sheriff Carson, Patrick says:

Dear Sheriff Carson:

I would appreciate your granting me a thirty-day leave of absence from my present position. I have accepted an investigative position in private industry and would like for the leave to become effective this date. As you know, I have received several offers from private industry and have decided to take one of these [sic.] I have enjoyed my association with this office, but I am unable to turn down this offer. It includes a higher salary and more chances for advancement.

With best regards I am sincerely,

James Calvin Patrick

The Jacksonville newspapers reported Patrick's newly acquired employment to be as the manager of the Wackenhut Corporation office in Jacksonville. The Wackenhut Corporation is a worldwide investigative and security agency. Chief Patrick's new employment and role with the Wackenhut Corporation will again be discussed in the chapter dealing with Governor Kirk's War on Crime.

J.C. Patrick would trouble Haydon Burns no more. Yet more heads would roll. William A. Hallowes indicted the previously exempted-from-prosecution senior officers

Woodrow Pruitt and Claude Bryant, III "by direct information." Direct information means that the charges were brought directly by the State Attorney. Tragically, Officer Bryant committed suicide before he could be brought to trial. Officer Pruitt was tried and convicted of breaking and entering and grand larceny. And sadly, the victimization of the two rookie officers continued. They were forced to offer up perjured testimony against Pruitt to protect Sheriff Carson, affirming that they had been working as undercover agents. The reader should be reminded that this perjured testimony was in direct conflict with their sworn court-reported confessions submitted to Governor Burns' investigators, February 1, 1965. When the defense counsel presented the content of the previous sworn confessions of the rookies, the explanation provided by the state was that those statements were not complete— evidently, the officers had forgotten or overlooked the fact they were undercover agents. This explanation defies all logic and reason and is baffling and difficult for a rational person to accept.

Shortly after the Pruitt trial, one of the rookies resigned from the Sheriff's Office. The other stayed with the Sheriff's Office until his retirement. [The author has purposely omitted the names of these rookies in this account because he and others consider them victims of Sheriff Carson's corruption believing the officers do not deserve negative notoriety.]

It is interesting to note that after Ron Johnson, owner of the Kenco Chemical Manufacturing Company, testified for the Sheriff's Office in the trial of Pruitt, he suffered no serious setbacks from the burglary of his facility. If fact, his company's shabby concrete-block manufacturing facility that was broken into — like Cinderella's pumpkin — soon blossomed into a larger manufacturing facility on West Beaver St in Jacksonville.

This facility began producing thousands upon thousands of gallons of Mr. Johnson's pesticide named, *Rid-A-Bug*. At the same time that Mr. Johnson moved his modest operation to the larger facility on Beaver Street in Jacksonville, his *Rid-A-Bug* product appeared on the shelves of hundreds of Winn-Dixie Stores throughout the Southeastern United States.

The sudden popularity of his pesticide resulted in Mr. Johnson becoming a very wealthy man. The following information is presented in the book solely for the readers to ponder. To borrow the motto of Fox News: *We report, you decide*. J.E. Davis, Sheriff Dale Carson's most personal, intimate friend, owned the Winn-Dixie stores. Carson's wife, Doris, was a highly regarded gynecologist who had helped Davis' wife through a critical illness and was credited by Mr. Davis with saving her life. That doctor/patient relationship had helped create the close friendship of the two men. Being aware of the Davis/Carson friendship, would it be fair to ask this question: If Duval County officers had not been apprehended breaking into the Kenco Chemical Manufacturing Company; would the company have experienced its sudden prosperity? Was the prosperity a reward for silence? Was there something favorable in Mr. Johnson's testimony that helped Sheriff Carson solidify the bogus undercover story? No one will ever know for the Pruitt trial transcript is missing from the official court trial records.

Whatever the reason for Ron Johnson's prosperity, it didn't hurt to know and be in the good will of Sheriff Carson and his powerful and wealthy friends did it?

Perhaps the product was good enough that it deserved the promotion it received in the Winn-Dixie stores. However, some professional exterminators interviewed said that if you sprayed an insect with *Funny*

Face Kool Aid, you'd kill it faster than you would with *Rid-A-Bug*.

Sadly, for the citizens of Florida and the people of our nation, Governor Burns joined Sheriff Carson in his criminal obstruction. Not only did Governor Burns allow Sheriff Carson to escape removal from office because of his personal involvement in the Kenco Chemical Manufacturing Company burglary cover-up, he also completely ignored taking any action against Sheriff Carson for the sheriff's criminal involvement in a multitude of other felonious acts. The details of these felonious acts were delivered personally to Governor Burns in the content of sworn affidavits on January 31, 1965 by a multitude of Duval County Sheriff's Office detectives—the same detectives he had appointed as special investigators.

For Governor Burns and Sheriff Carson, this whole scenario was quite a magic show—to make confessed burglars disappear and then reappear as undercover agents is quite a performance, equal to what one might see in Las Vegas where things disappear before one's eyes.

Chapter Fourteen:
Suspension

Just because you're paranoid
doesn't mean they aren't after you
.--Kurt Cobain

Work continued as usual for Sergeants Cody, Coleman, West, and Lieutenant Ray Headen, but their little island of peace would be short-lived, for Sheriff Carson was not through with them. The first sign that danger was lurking nearby was revealed in <u>June of 1965</u> when Duval County Patrolman Fred Geer visited Sergeant Cody at his residence.

"I'm really concerned, Lee about something that's happened," Geer said. "I was summoned to the second floor and was asked to reopen a case I had investigated."

Though Officer Geer would not identify *who* summoned him, Cody knew that the phrase "second floor" was used as a euphemism for Sheriff Carson's personal office.

Patrolman Geer went on to explain that the case was against two juveniles—Bruce Cox, the seventeen-year-old son of John Cox, the attorney for the Civil Service Board—and another juvenile, David Reddick. The juveniles had snatched a purse from Mrs. Elizabeth Hunter. The purse contained her keys and $1.50 in cash. The boys were apprehended shortly after the purse snatching, and the next day Mrs. Hunter met with the Patrolmen Geer, the juveniles and their parents.

The parents of the juveniles and Mrs. Hunter reached an agreement that Mrs. Hunter would not press charges. Mrs. Hunter was evidently a compassionate woman and concluded that the boys had learned their lesson and thinking of their future, decided to let the parents address the discipline of the boys. This was a generous decision, for at this time in Florida robbery was a felony that carried a life sentence. With Officer Geer in total agreement the boys were remanded to their parents and the complainant, as agreed, never sought prosecution.

Officer Geer went on to reveal how he refused to become involved in the matter again, explaining that this was in his judgment a minor incident and to reopen the case would be inappropriate and unwarranted. There would be no logical or legal reason to press these belated charges against the juveniles, especially since the complainant had declined to prosecute the young men.

Sheriff Carson did not agree.

Officer Geer, fully cognizant as was the rest of the sheriff's office of Sheriff Carson's campaign to discredit and destroy Governor Burns's investigators Cody, Coleman and West, said he felt Sheriff Carson was using this situation to intimidate Civil Service Board attorney John Cox by bringing unwarranted charges of robbery against his juvenile son. "I just wanted to warn you guys," he said. "I put two and two together and I'm sure Sheriff Carson is up to something very unlawful."

Officer Geer had no idea at the time how totally accurate his prediction would prove to be. Shortly after warning Cody, Geer resigned from the Sheriff's Office and returned to his home in West Florida.

On <u>June 16, 1965</u>, according to a sworn statement submitted by Elizabeth Hunter, Duval County Sergeants J.L. Suber and Matthew Kemp appeared unannounced at Mrs. Hunter's residence. They advised her that State Attorney Hallowes had reviewed the purse-snatching incident and decided that the case against the juveniles should not have been dropped and should now be prosecuted. They asked her to accompany them to the office of the Justice of the Peace where she could sign an affidavit so that the judge could issue a robbery warrant for the juveniles.

Mrs. Hunter said she saw no reason to do that. In her mind, the matter had been satisfactorily settled between her and the juveniles' parents months ago.

The detectives left, but returned twice that same day and were even more earnest and insistent that she go with them in the interest of justice. Knowing that Sheriff Carson was a powerful man, she became afraid, and fearing that something bad could happen to herself or to her family if she did not cooperate, she finally relented and reluctantly accompanied the detectives to the Office of Justice of the Peace Jessie Leigh.

There, Mrs. Hunter was presented a blank printed form identified as an affidavit, which she was asked to sign. She reminded the detectives again that she had agreed to not prosecute the juveniles in April of 1965, and that she did not understand why the matter was even raised for discussion three months later. When she asked what should be on the blank lines of the affidavit, she was told to not worry about it, that the judge would fill that in later. Sergeant Suber continued to pressure her and insist that she sign the affidavit.

She signed the document.

On June 18, 1965, Judge Leigh then issued a warrant for the arrest of the juveniles, Bruce Cox and David Reddick. On July 16, 1965, State Attorney William A. Hallowes formally charge Bruce Cox with robbery via direct information. On August 3, 1965, Mildred and John

Cox were notified that their son would be arraigned in Division A Criminal Court for the felony crime of robbery.

On <u>August 4, 1965</u>, the new lieutenants Grant and Fleming dropped their legal quest to stop the new Civil Service Exam for Detective Lieutenant. The detectives naively may have thought that Fleming and Grant had seen the error of their ways and the futility of their cause. Actually, Sheriff Carson had something else up his sleeve, another means to keep the irritating detectives in line and without promotion. On <u>August 24, 1965</u>, Bruce Cox was arraigned on the felony charge of robbery.

The Civil Service Board met again in Executive Session on <u>August 26</u> and designated <u>September 15, 1965</u> as the new date for the promotional exam for Detective Lieutenant. The Civil Service Board also ruled that the fraudulent progress reports utilized previously would not be considered in the scheduled <u>September 15</u> exam when compiling the final exam grades as was done in the prior exam.

On <u>August 27, 1965</u>, only one day after the good news of a new test date, Sergeants Cody, Coleman, West and Lt. Headen were suspended by Sheriff Dale Carson for thirty days without pay with recommendation that their employment be terminated from the Sheriff's Office at the end of the suspension period. This termination request made these officers, who had exposed the prior fraudulent exam and participated in Governor Burns' investigation of Sherriff Carson, automatically terminated if the Civil Service Board found that the rules violations alleged in the suspension complaint were for just cause.

<u>Note</u>: Lieutenant Ray Headen was added to Sheriff Carson's hit list and was suspended along with the detectives. Lieutenant Headen had been an outspoken supporter of the detectives from the beginning, and Sheriff

Carson had rightly interpreted Headen's stance as disloyal and a threat to his ability to continue as sheriff of Duval County. Lt. Headen's suspension outraged many officers. Headen was well-liked and highly respected man in the law enforcement community and throughout Duval County. Adding salt to the wound, Lt. Headen was *only six months away from retirement*.

There was also another factor that certainly helped cause Lieutenant Headen's suspension: With the resignation of Chief Patrick, Lieutenant Headen would be one of the two detective lieutenants eligible to fill the office of Chief of Detectives. Certainly, Sheriff Carson could not allow an officer like Lieutenant Headen, who had openly condemned the crimes and behavior of the sheriff to occupy this important position. The only other detective eligible for the position was Lieutenant James Hamlin, the head of Duval County Sheriff's Office Vice Squad. His office adjoined the second floor office of Sheriff Carson, and he was known to be one of Carson's loyal soldiers and cronies. Hamlin was the officer that accompanied Chief Patrick to his mother's home in Atlanta at the behest of the Sherriff. The details of that trip were explained in an earlier chapter.

The detectives appealed the suspensions and according the Civil Service Board set a suspension/dismissal appeal hearing for October 4, 1965.

The detectives subpoenaed their witnesses and by September 30, all subpoenas were successfully served with the exception of former Detective Chief J.C. Patrick, a critical witness for the defense. Notes made on Patrick's subpoena indicated he could not be found within the bounds of Duval County, though records proved he and his family had lived at the same address at Neptune Beach for over a decade and had not moved.

On October 4, the requested hearing was held. All four officers were found *not guilty* as charged. However, acting on Attorney Cox's legal advice, the Civil Service

123

Board upheld the thirty-day suspension stating that the officers had already served the suspension making it and the punitive pay loss a moot question. This was the legal hook that Sheriff Carson needed. On this date Civil Service Board Attorney John Cox and Civil Service Board Member John Griner delivered that hook on a silver platter.

Carson immediately filed a "Writ of Certiorari," seeking review of a court's decision in a higher court. Judge Roger Waybright responded by ruling that the Civil Service Board had erred in upholding the suspensions then finding the officers not guilty. Judge Waybright then ordered the officers dismissed from employment.

After the circuit court ruling Civil Service Board Chairman Carl Taylor became suspicious that justice was being obstructed. He then contacted the detective's legal counsel and reveled the following. During the suspension appeal hearings, according to Board Chairman Taylor, after reaching a consensus that they did not wish for Sheriff Carson to terminate the detectives, Board member John Griner posed this question to John Cox, the attorney for the Civil Service Board. "Mr. Cox, I hate to make the Sheriff look so bad. Can't we uphold the suspension and still find the detectives not guilty?"

Attorney Cox answered without hesitation.

"Certainly."

Carl Taylor pressed the issue. "Are you sure the rules will allow that?"

Attorney Cox again expressed his absolute certainty. "Oh, yes, no problem."

Because of Chairman Carl Taylor's revelations the detectives were now convinced that a conspiracy that had cost them their jobs was in bloom and at this point petals of the conspiratorial flower bore the names of Sheriff Dale Carson, State Attorney William A. Hallowes, III, Civil Service Board

Attorney John Cox and Civil Service Board Member John Griner.

   To assist in understanding the detectives concerns that a conspiracy existed consider the following facts:

1. On October 6, just three days after Cox gave flawed legal advice to the Civil Service Board. Co-conspirator Hallowes delivered on time. The felony charges against the son of Attorney John Cox were reduced On October 7 to petit larceny and placed on the absentee docket. These reduced charges were *Nol Prossed* (dropped) on April 26, 1966. The unwarranted indictment against Cox's son, had served its useful purpose. And though Cox's cooperation with Sheriff Carson was illegal and immoral, it is understandable. Any devoted father would likely do the same thing, even if it were illegal or immoral, to keep his son out of prison and deliver him from people who had the power and will to do whatever evil they wanted.

2. Civil Service Board Member John Griner was an employee of Gordon Thompson Chevrolet in the lease department. Gordon Thompson Chevrolet leased a million dollars worth of vehicles to the Sheriff's Office every year—an impressive contract and the lease renewal bid was due in approximately two months. Somehow Gordon Thompson Chevrolet always prevailed as the low bidder.

3. The mother of Civil Service Board Member Warren Thomas had been arrested for DWI in November of 1965 and Leaving the Scene of an Accident after Causing Bodily Injury to another. This felony offense was reduced to a misdemeanor On December 15, 1965. State Attorney Hallowes delivers on time, again. This offence reduction date was just one day before Civil Service Board Member Thomas was to render his "Not

to Appeal" vote. Months later the punishment Board Member Thomas' mother received for her felony offence was a $200 fine.

4. Paul Akin was one of two outside property appraisers employed by Duval County Property Appraiser's Office. Thus, he derived a substantial portion of his income directly from the coffers of Duval County. In addition, his daughter was married to attorney Thomas Green, brother of Attorney C. Ray Green, a close personal friend of Sheriff Carson and a well-known power broker.

At this juncture, after the Circuit Court decision that terminated their employment, the detectives requested that the Civil Service Board appeal the Circuit Court decision. A hearing was held on December 16, 1965. Subsequently, after deliberation, Board Members Griner, Thomas and Akin voted not to appeal the Court's action giving the conspirators the majority votes to prevail. This decision by Board Members Griner, Thomas and Akin was a blatant illegal violation of the Civil Service Act, a statute law. It was the inescapable duty and obligation of these elected officials to protect employees Cody, Coleman, West and Headen, not to enable the illegal termination of their employment to stand.

NOTE: *In 1975 the United States Supreme Court held it unconstitutional to punitively administer to an employee without first allowing a hearing to determine just cause. In this case that is exactly what happened to the officers. Their civil rights had been flagrantly violated. Subsequent to this ruling this author made both federal and state offices obligated by oath of office aware of this Supreme Court decision. As of the publication date of this book no attempt has been made by any state or federal official who knew or should have known to assist the violated officers.*

It is not hard to understand the three Civil Service Board Members "Not to Appeal" decision. The "Not to Appeal" vote eliminated any opportunity for the terminated

126

detectives to have a legal standing. The "Not to Appeal" vote by Board Members Griner, Thomas and Akin should solidify the beyond all doubt in anyone's mind the existence of the conspiracy so feared by the violated detectives.

These "Not to Appeal" votes now add two more names to the petals of the conspiratorial flower: Civil Service Board Members Warren Thomas and Paul Akin. The conspiratorial flower was now in full bloom.

There is one other factor to consider when analyzing what precipitated Civil Service Board Members Griner, Thomas and Akin "Not to Appeal" votes other than their conspiratorial obligation.

Consider this; if the detectives had been reinstated they would have had their powers of arrest restored. I think it is fair to say the conspirators all feared that eventuality. This author, one of their victims, can assure the readers that the conspirator's fearful concerns were well founded.

To make the just revealed unchallengeable acts of criminal conspiracy more egregious, officers, both federal and state, warranted by oath of office to punish the conspirators chose to ignore from 1965 to present the furnished, documented readily available evidence of the conspiracy thereby allowing four dedicated police officers to remain victims of the reported documented corruption.

Chapter Fifteen:
Still Seeking Justice

Justice denied anywhere diminishes
justice everywhere.
—Martin Luther King

In 1966, the detectives were still searching for vindication and an avenue of justice. CBS Channel Four (JXTV) in Jacksonville initiated an investigation of the city commissioners and city councilmen of the City of Jacksonville. This investigative effort was headed by a seasoned investigative reported by the name of Alpheus B. Parsons. Parsons was a Korean War veteran, having spent his nineteenth birthday on Heartbreak Ridge. He had worked with a paper in Mount Dora, Florida, and had earned the prestigious International Gold Quill Award awarded for his journalistic excellence. Parsons' boldness epitomized the spirit of Martin Luther King, Jr. who said, "Speak without fear."

Parsons' investigative efforts resulted in the indictment and conviction of several Jacksonville city commissioners and councilmen. Encouraged by Parsons' fruitful investigative effort, Sergeant Cody decided to call upon Al Parsons and request that he investigate Sheriff Dale Carson, other members of the Sheriff's Office, and State Fourth Judicial Attorney William A. Hallowes, III. Parsons said that he would more than happy to receive any documented evidence that would prove the existence of corruption in the Sheriff's Office or the State Attorney's Office.

Lee Cody then provided Parsons with the story of Johnnie Mae Chappell, a mass of documents related to that conspiracy, more documents relating to other instances of corruption and obstruction of justice committed by Sheriff Carson, Chief Patrick, and State Attorney William A. Hallowes, III, as well as an extensive witness list. It was basically the same evidence that had been turned over to Governor Burns in 1965, evidence that had been ignored and covered up. Al Parsons promised to review the documents and witness list and get back in touch with Cody as soon as possible.

Approximately three days later, Parsons asked Cody to meet him for a conference at TV Channel Four. For the lack of a better adjective, Parsons was *stunned* by the evidence he had reviewed. He said he wanted to immediately initiate an investigation into Sheriff Carson's office as well as that of William A. Hallowes, III. Parsons solicited Cody's help and guidance in the investigation. Parsons seemed particularly bothered by the gravity of the corruption in State Attorney Hallowes' office and the protection Hallowes had afforded to state and county officials. Parsons had his own concerns. He related to Cody the details of the trivial charges State Attorney Hallowes had made against City Council Chairman Lemuel Sharp, Sr., a case that Parsons had repeatedly tried to persuade the State Attorney to drop. Parsons said, "I don't understand it. It seems that State Attorney Hallowes and his first assistant Edward Booth had a burning desire to prosecute Councilman Sharp. I feel there must be some personal animosity between the them." Parsons explained that the reason he had tried to dissuade Hallowes from prosecuting Sharp was that the only questionable thing he had uncovered about Sharp was that the councilman had purchased a door from a Jacksonville glass company to be installed on his city council building on Pearl Street that was being remodeled. The building was owned by Councilman Sharp, but was leased to the city and used for city offices. This door had been purchased through the city's Recreational Department, and by doing this, Sharp had taken advantage of a 20% discount the company offered to city officials and employees.

Hallowes viewed this as a crime because the door had not been paid for and energetically set out to convict Sharp.

In Parson's opinion, the door had not been paid for because Sharp had not been billed in a timely fashion and Hallowes determination to prosecute Sharp seemed harsh and unfair. Almost all city employees had utilized the city discount for decades, and some for amounts that far exceeded the cost of the door Sharp had purchased to use on city-leased property.

Cody agreed with Parson's opinion that Sharp did not deserve the treatment he received, as he had personally known Mr. Sharp and his family for many years. It was well known throughout Duval County that Lemuel Sharp had done more for the City of Jacksonville and its citizens than any other politician who had occupied an office there. Cody told Parsons that Sharp was known to have a golden heart and to not have a greedy or malicious bone in his body and would never consider deliberately violating the law.

Parsons went on to say that because of what he had learned from Cody about Hallowes corruption, he could not reconcile the fact that Hallowes and his first assistant Eddie Booth, particularly Booth, was so vehement about prosecuting Sharp over the belated billing of an office door. It was especially difficult to understand since he had furnished documented, irrefutable evidence of criminal acts perpetuated by Mayor Louis Ritter that State Attorney Hallowes had refused to act upon.

Sadly, even though after appealing his conviction claiming the state had withheld critical evidence and being granted a new trial Councilman Sharp, because of his age and the expense of an extended legal contest, pled guilty to the grand larceny charge and was given a two-year probation. Cody said Mr. Sharp certainly did not deserve that maltreatment.

Parsons said that if he had known of Hallowes' extensive malfeasance, he would never have involved himself in the investigation of the City of Jacksonville officials and would have walked away from the assignment. Parsons said he did not recognize it at first, but now he strongly believes the investigation of the city officials was precipitated by the local power structure so that they could implement consolidation and gain control of the city.

About three days later, Parsons contacted Cody and asked to meet again. In this meeting, Parsons said, "I approached my General Manager [Glenn Marshal] and shared the documented evidence you provided me against Sheriff Carson and State Attorney Hallowes. He absolutely refused to allow me to continue the investigation. He said, 'Absolutely not. You cannot investigate Sheriff Carson or the office of State Attorney Hallowes.' His flawed rationale was that if we get rid of them, we might get someone worse. I told him we couldn't get anybody worse in either office and he ought to be ashamed of himself for voicing such a thing."

Cody could tell that Parsons was infuriated by this cover-up. Not long after confronting his manager, Al Parsons received his marching orders and he was transferred to a sister television station in Kansas City, Missouri.

Chapter Sixteen:
Governor Kirk and His War on Crime

This is Claude Kirk, Governor of Florida.
Do you read my press? Then you know that
I'm a tree-shakin' son of a bitch.
—Claude Kirk

In 1967, Claude Kirk was elected as Florida's governor, the first Republican to hold the office in ninety years, since Reconstruction. He was a former Marine, serving in both WWII and the Korean War. Wealthy and flamboyant, this graduate of the University of Alabama School of Law used much of his own resources to finance his famous War on Crime campaign. Because Florida had no state police organization at that time that could operate independently throughout the state, Kirk retained the Wackenhut Corporation, an international security and investigative firm, headed by George Wackenhut, a retired FBI agent, to be his investigative arm for his War on Crime, which targeted public corruption.

Cody and his fellow detectives had not given up their quest for justice, but they were fighting discouragement. One day as they discussed Kirk's War on Crime and how Kirk's campaign might help vindicate them and help them expose the extensive criminality they knew existed in Duval County, Claude West said, "I see Bill Eddy now and then in the course of my duties. [West was then employed as a Florida livestock inspector] I bet he can find out how we can contact an agent of the War on

Crime." Bill Eddy was a state beverage agent, and Claude West had previously been in charge of State Beverage Law Enforcement for Duval County. West and Eddy were friends and had often worked together on cases.

Claude West contacted Bill Eddy who arranged for West and Cody to meet with Al Healy, an executive with the Wackenhut organization.

Bill Eddy informed Al Healy that the detectives had information on corruption in the Duval County Sheriff's Office and the Fourth Judicial State Attorney's Office. Mr. Healey would be glad to receive that information but surprisingly, Healy first desired to know what the detectives knew about J.C. Patrick who had recently been employed as their office manager in Jacksonville. Healy said Patrick had been highly recommended by Sheriff Dale Carson.

Cody and the others related every instance of Patrick's corruption which they had knowledge. Cody also shared how he had learned from his former riding partner, Sergeant John Britts, who was a former Jacksonville Beach police officer that Britts had arrested Patrick for indecent exposure and being publicly drunk and disorderly. Patrick was a Jacksonville Beach bartender at the time.

Mr. Healy was visibly taken aback by the revelation of Patrick's actions and character. "I am sure Mr. Wackenhut will be interested in learning this, and he's going to be appalled because Patrick was hired on the basis of the strong recommendations of Sheriff Dale Carson. We'll be in touch with you."

Shortly thereafter, two War on Crime investigators— Willis Benner and Gene Joyce, both former FBI employees— contacted the detectives and asked if they could meet them at their Jacksonville motel room. Agents Benner and Joyce indicated they were primarily interested in first learning more about Patrick's Jacksonville Beach arrest. Agent Benner said that Patrick had claimed on his employment application that he had never been arrested.

Cody said, "We can take you to the arresting officer." Cody explained that Britts had formerly worked for the Jacksonville Beach Police but was now a detective sergeant with the Duval County Sheriff's Office. The War on Crime agents and former detectives did meet with Sergeant Britts who verified the time, date, place and cause of Patrick's arrest. Agents Benner and Joyce proceeded to the Jacksonville Beach Police Department, and after informing Chief Charles Franks that they were agents for Governor Kirk's War on Crime, made further inquiry into Patrick's arrest, supplying Franks with the details Britts provided.

After an hour's wait, Franks returned and said, "We can find no record of J.C. Patrick ever being arrested at Jacksonville Beach on any date."

Agent Benner rather firmly said, "Chief, we believe our information is valid. Would you please check again? We're going to lunch and then we'll be back to see what you've found."

When they returned, Chief Franks said, "Well, what do you know. We found it. Patrick was indeed arrested on that date and Officer John Britts was the arresting officer. I apologize for not finding it earlier."

Benner took the copy of the arrest report and said, "Thank you. We're returning to Miami, but when we return to Jacksonville, we'll be in touch."

Two days later, Benner contacted West and Cody and said, "Mr. Wackenhut was infuriated when he learned about Patrick's arrest and criminal activity. He was also very disappointed in Dale Carson for recommending him and distressed by what he's learned about Dale Carson's own criminal activities. He also immediately discharged Patrick. Mr. Wackenhut then recommended to Governor Kirk that the governor launch a full-scale criminal investigation of the Duval County Sheriff's Office and the Fourth Judicial State Attorney's Office of William A. Hallowes, III."

Agent Benner indicated that Mr. Wackenhut wanted former detectives Cody and West to assist in the investigation. For weeks, Cody and West worked hand in hand with Wackenhut's investigators, each witness that West and Cody provided and each account of corruption led to another. Within two months, twenty-two boxes (14 cubic feet) of files, documents, sworn depositions of scores of witnesses and other evidence were gathered. The witnesses included convicted felons as well as politicians and former and present employees of the Duval County Sheriff's Office.

At this point, Benner decided that enough evidence had been collected and they could begin prosecution. The next step would be to ask the attorney for the War on Crime —Shelby Highsmith [currently a sitting Federal judge in Miami]—to meet with them, evaluate their evidence and make his legal recommendations to George Wackenhut.

Shelby Highsmith communicated his findings to George Wackenhut, the Director for the Governor's War on Crime, in a four-page letter dated September 22, 1967:

Highsmith says, "No attempt will be made here to detail the many incidents of corruption and illegal activity uncovered by the investigation." The intensity of Highsmith's language is indicative of the corruption the detectives had exposed. For example he says, "For the past several years the county jail has been a cesspool of illegal activity." About the Sheriff's Office he says, "there is evidence of widespread illegal activity on the part of members of the Sheriff's Road Patrol. These activities include 'pay-offs' in D.W.I. cases, conversion of county property, and alteration of official records." He concludes the letter by saying, "Because of the multitude of problems, and the number of persons and officers implicated, further pure investigation will serve little purpose. It is, in my opinion, absolutely essential that a special prosecutor be assigned." Highsmith was convinced that Sheriff Carson was involved in illegal activity so he suggested that Carson not be informed of these findings and conclusions. About Attorney Hallowes' possible involvement in the Duval County corruption, Highsmith says, "It is also recommended that the Grand Jury be utilized in the investigation of the State Attorney's office and the instances of judicial misconduct."

Highsmith's recommendations were presented to Wackenhut, who in turn presented them to Governor Kirk. Kirk in turn named State Attorney Charles Carlton from St. Lucie County as a special prosecutor. Kirk directed Carlton to counsel with War on Crime agents Benner and Joyce and the Foreman of the Duval County Grand Jury, for the purpose of examining and reviewing the documented evidence in preparation for presentation and prosecution to a grand jury. Special Prosecutor Carlton and his chief investigator Robert Knowles proceeded to Duval County and began the immediate processing of charges.

The detectives were ecstatic. At last, it seemed like they would be vindicated and the corrupt powers who had manhandled Duval County for decades, who had illegally committed criminal obstruction of justice in the murder investigation of Johnnie Mae Chappell and had illegally terminated their employment would at last be forced to stand before the bar of justice themselves.

The detectives' hopes were again dashed without warning. Special Prosecutor Carlton advised Cody, West, and Coleman that Governor Kirk had advised him he wanted the Duval County investigation to cease immediately. Carlton was dismayed and displayed disbelief. Carlton apologized but could offer no explanation to the detectives as to why Kirk had closed down the investigation and prosecution. All legal proceedings relating to the War on Crime in Duval County were terminated. This happened in spite of pleas from Sergeants West, Cody, and Coleman as well as Grand Jury Foreman Edward F. Sullivan, who in a telegram forwarded to Governor Claude Kirk on February 26, 1968, requested, "additional state investigative personnel be dispatched to Duval County immediately." Sullivan warned that dire consequences to the investigation would follow if the requested additional personnel were not sent.

Governor Kirk ignored the pleas of the Grand Jury foreman. Special Prosecutor Carlton and his investigator Robert Knowles displayed discouraged disbelief and returned to St. Lucie County. Without the help and backing of the governor, nothing could be accomplished by the grand jury.

What had happened? In a scene reminiscent of what had occurred with Governor Burns, Governor Kirk summoned Dale Carson to Tallahassee. The Jacksonville *Folio,* an extremely popular weekly publication, published an article written by Susan Clark Armstrong entitled "Meet the Sheriff" claims that Kirk also met privately with J.E. Davis and J. Ashley Verlander. It should be pointed out again that J.E. Davis (Winn-Dixie, the great distributor of *Rid-A-Bug*) was a close friend and personal confidant of Sheriff Carson.

In a letter to Governor Askew's office, Al Parsons, award-winning journalist and former investigative reporter for Channel Four, says he learned that J.E. Davis intervened and that his influence was the major reason Governor Kirk did not remove Sheriff Carson from office. There seems to be substance to Parson's claim. On September 11, 1956, Claude Kirk and J. Ashley Verlander formed a corporation known as the American Heritage Life Insurance Company. J.E. Davis had provided most of the starter funds and became a major stockholder. As a result of this business enterprise, Claude Kirk became a very wealthy man.

The aforementioned *Folio Weekly* article contains several quotations from Shelby Highsmith that are relevant. For example, beneath a photo of Highsmith is this tag:

Shelby Highsmith, now a federal judge in Miami, conducted the 1967 probe of Carson's JSO [Jacksonville Sheriff's Office] and found corruption so pervasive he urged the governor to exclude local law enforcement from the investigation. Instead the governor turned the matter over to one of the people [State Attorney Hallowes] implicated in Highsmith's report.

Highsmith and Carlton were not the only ones dismayed at the news of the halted War on Crime investigation in Duval County. Agent Benner called Claude West and asked that he and Cody meet him. He said he had something he needed to tell them and he also wanted to furnish them a document that would perhaps help them with their quest for justice in the future. Benner met with the detectives at the intersection of Spring Glen and Spring Park roads in Jacksonville.

Benner told the detectives that he and the majority of the former FBI agents who had been assigned to work with Kirk's War on Crime (including Gene Joyce) had just resigned in disgust. When they learned that Kirk had called off the War on Crime investigation and prosecutions in

Duval County and that the criminal activities of Sheriff Carson, J.C. Patrick, and State Attorney Hallowes would remain unexposed and unpunished, it was more than they could live with.

Agent Benner went on to reveal that he was in George Wackenhut's office when Wackenhut reached the governor by telephone. After cursing Governor Kirk furiously, Mr. Wackenhut stated in no uncertain terms, "Governor, you are a disgrace to our state and our nation for covering up the criminality that our agents have uncovered in Duval County. And from this moment on, neither me nor my agency will be affiliated in any way with the office of the governor or your so-called War on Crime." He then abruptly hung up the phone.

Investigative journalist Al Parsons says that for State Attorney William A. Hallowes, III, "Justice is not a blindfold but a cash register." When State Attorney Hallowes finally retired, Governor Kirk appointed T. Edward Austin as State Attorney. Austin was a man who would prove to be as equally corrupt as his predecessor.

In 1969, when Austin was first appointed, the former detectives again were apprehensive. They had all known him when he had served as Public Defender. They also thought it strange that a Republican governor would appoint a Democrat to the prestigious and powerful position of State Attorney. They were also of the opinion that Governor Kirk would never appoint a state attorney to the Fourth Judicial Circuit who would pursue and prosecute the officials and law enforcement officers exposed by his War on Crime in 1967. If Kirk did not have this guarantee, the thwarted investigation would certainly come back to haunt him.

Soon after State Attorney Austin's appointment in 1969 and still desperate for justice, the former detectives informed Austin and his staff that Governor Kirk's War on Crime in 1967 had incriminated scores of individuals, including many high-ranking public officials, and that because of the governor's order to halt the investigation, the criminals were still at large. They pointed out that many prosecutions prepared by Attorney Carlton that were pending were never completed or presented to the Grand Jury.

The former detectives presented State Attorney Austin with a letter from War on Crime attorney Shelby Highsmith provided to them by resigned War on Crime agent Willis Benner. The detectives hope that the letter's contents would hopefully erase any doubts Austin might have had about the motives of the former detectives. The former detectives told State Attorney Austin that there was a massive amount of evidence collected somewhere, either in the possession of the Wackenhut corporation or hidden somewhere in the Florida state archives.

Making Austin aware of Highsmith's letter and how much information had been gathered in the original research was an error and would later turn out to be a serious tactical mistake.

Attorney Austin, like governors Burns, Kirk, and his predecessor William A. Hallowes, III, chose to obstruct justice rather than fulfill the duties of his office.

Chapter Seventeen:
Governor Askew

*In 1974 Governor Askew was named by
TIME magazine as one of the
200 Faces for the Future.*

In 1975, Reubin O'Donovan Askew was elected governor of Florida. In that same year, Alpheus B. Parsons returned to Duval County. The feisty and award-winning investigative reporter contacted Lee Cody and Claude West. He told them he was going to start a weekly publication in Jacksonville named *The Citizen* and that he was still devastated over the fact that Sheriff Carson, Fourth Judicial State Attorneys Hallowes, Austin and other Duval County officials had escaped exposure and prosecution for their criminal conduct. Parsons intended to use his newspaper as a vehicle to expose corruption and once again attempt to administer justice in Duval County.

In addition to starting the newspaper, Parsons continued his crusade by sending a minority report he had prepared to Governor Askew. It actually was the same minority report that he had previously sent to Governor Kirk, who had ignored its contents. Parsons was not a stranger to those in government. In fact, he was known and respected for his speech writing. He had written speeches for Richard Nixon and even previous speeches for Reuben Askew. In his cover letter to Governor Askew, Parsons said:

I have enclosed the first edition of my weekly newspaper for your scrutiny. Some of us in Duval

County are seeking relief from what has been an untenable situation. This matter has been brought to the attention of previous governors who have found it politically expedient not to prosecute the matter. We feel certain that you are made of sterner stuff.

Parson's minority report is a focal point in the discussion of the corruption and criminal activities taking place in Duval County. This eighteen-page report, now in Cody's possession, is in Parson's words, "both an accusation and an appeal: We accuse these men and others of corrupting their offices, and we appeal to you for justice, something which is not a birthright in Duval County." Lee Cody had known justice had fled Duval County ever since the Johnnie Mae Chappell murder.

When Parsons had worked for WJXT Channel 4 in Jacksonville, his investigative work exposed extensive and virulent corruption in almost every area of city and county government. Yet, he was unable to accomplish what he wanted—to see justice served. For example, when he aired a special report charging widespread corruption in the county jail, station management refused to allow him to pursue the matter and allowed Sheriff Dale Carson airtime to refute each and every allegation that Parson's witnesses had sworn to. The station management would not allow any of Parson's witnesses to appear at the station to verify their assertions.

Parsons did not blindside government officials with the strong articles in his newspaper. In fact, he went out of his way to inform officials in writing what he planned to publish. For example, he wrote Art Canady, Legal Counsel for Governor Askew and said, "I want to keep the Governor's office appraised of the information I intend to publish in upcoming issues of my new weekly newspaper in Duval County to be called THE CITIZEN."

Lee Cody also wrote to Governor Askew, and like Parsons, did not receive a response to his letters. In fact, Cody was still having difficulty finding any responsible public official who was concerned about the criminal obstruction of justice prevalent in the investigation of Johnnie Mae Chappell's murder, the prosecution of her assailants, and the trashing of the careers of the detectives who had attempted to bring her murderers to justice.

In Cody's possession is a January 6, 1975 letter from Ed Austin to Donald M. Middlebrooks. In this letter, Attorney Ed Austin is assuring Middlebrooks, the Assistant General Counsel to Governor Askew, that he had no intention of acting upon Al Parson's minority report and reopening any facet of the allegations of criminal activity in Duval County. He states that the allegations are "without legal substance."

State Attorney Austin had by this point definitely established himself as an adversary to both Parsons and Cody and an ally to Sheriff Carson. About his relationship and close friendship with Dale Carson, Ed Austin says:

This respect arises in part from the fact that Sheriff Carson would immediately carry out his professional responsibility to investigate any wrongdoing by me or any member of my staff just as we would most assuredly expect our office to carry out our responsibilities in any dealings with his [Sheriff Carson's] department.

Cody believes these words written by State Attorney T. Edward Austin to be intentional, unequivocal lies. Here is a profound example of why. The following information is taken from a sworn deposition given by former Florida Highway Patrol Officer Danny Howard.

On the night of November 3 and the morning of November 4, 1974, a Jacksonville Sheriff's Office detective, Ronald Kennerly, was off-duty and driving around with Danny Howard, his roommate. They drove an ABAR (Anti-Burglary and Robbery) vehicle assigned to Kennerly. After a quick stop at Jax Liquors drive-through window, the pair crossed the Matthews Bridge, running the tollgate, heading west into Jacksonville. Howard said Kennerly was running about eighty miles an hour. Suddenly, Kennerly exclaimed, "I think I'll go downtown and shoot up the NAACP building. Howard, thinking Kennerly was joking, said, "I think that's a good idea."

However, instead of shooting up the NAACP building, Kennerly decided to shoot up a black housing project known as Blodgett Homes.

Interestingly enough, at that time, Leroy Butler, who would later become Florida State All-American and an All-Pro football star with the Green Bay Packers, lived in the Blodgett housing project. Kennerly indiscriminately discharged his firearm as they drove up one street and down another, striking vehicles and God knows what else. According to a *Folio Weekly* article entitled "Shots in the Dark," written by Susan Armstrong and relating this same story in greater detail, Kennerly was "screaming like a wild animal."

Kennerly switched his police radio frequency to Zone 3, where the Blodgett Project was located, and monitored the radio. Kennerly was highly amused at the number of citizens calling in for assistance and listening to the reports of the "beat" (marked) police cars looking for him.

Officer Howard, according to his own sworn words, said that at one point he grabbed at Kennerly's arm. Officer Kennerly pointed his weapon at Howard and said, "You better not fuck with me."

Officer Howard ceased and just settled back for wherever this wild ride would take him. The officers proceeded east across the Matthews Bridge toward a bedroom community known as Arlington.

Upon arrival in Arlington, at a shopping center they rendezvoused with PIC (Patrolman in Charge) Sergeant Jack Jones. Officer Kennerly told Sergeant Jones that he had just shot up "nigger town" and was laughing. Kennerly said he felt like shooting up Arlington and asked if he could borrow Jones .44 magnum revolver. PIC Sergeant Jones, also thinking Kennerly was joking, handed him the pistol. Howard remained with Jones while Kennerly drove away.

Officer Kennerly then proceeded to an Arlington bar called Crabshaws and indiscriminately fired through the front door and window. Then Kennerly proceeded to another Arlington bar and pool hall named Guys & Dolls. He again fired indiscriminately into the business, again through the front door and window. Kennerly then returned to the Town & Country shopping center, returned the .44 magnum to PIC Officer Jones. Jones was ordered by radio to investigate the Arlington shootings. The three rode in Jones' car and admired Kennerly's handiwork. Jones then returned Kennerly and Howard to Kennerly's vehicle and Kennerly transported Officer Danny Howard to the apartment they were sharing.

Officer Kennerly then proceeded to the home of Jim Lucas and his wife, owners of Guys & Dolls. The Lucas home was located on Hiedi Road in Arlington, discharged an Uzzi (Israeli) machinegun into the Lucas vehicle parked in the driveway. He also fired into the front bedroom window, where their infant was asleep in her crib.

Then Kennerly stopped his reign of terror—at least for that night.

On April 3, 1979, Alpheus Parsons and Lee Cody hand-delivered to State Attorney T. Edward Austin the court-reported sworn deposition, tendered by former

147

Florida Highway Patrol officer Danny Howard. This deposition described the events that Howard witnessed with his own eyes on the night of November 3 and the morning of November 4, actions perpetrated by terrorist Jacksonville Sheriff Office Detective, Ron Kennerly.

Howard says that in July of 1975, Officer Ron Kennerly's terrorist rampage was "made known to my superiors in the Florida Highway Patrol, which resulted in my being summoned to the State Attorney's office." Within the sworn deposition they took from him, on page nine, is the following excerpt: "And then I talked with the State Attorney's Office, explained to them *exactly* what happened and they told me that they would probably want, if they prosecuted Kennerly, to use me as state witness."

Witness Howard never heard from the State Attorney's Office again nor was he ever summoned to a grand jury as a witness.

When Officer Howard's deposition was made public, on April 4, 1979, State Attorney Austin issued a press release stating that his testimony had been given to a grand jury. Steve Crosby quotes Austin in an article in the Florida Times-Union. Crosby says Austin claimed that "although the case against Kennerly looked good at first glance, it was weak. He said there were no corroborating witnesses. And he said ballistics tests failed to tie any of the spent bullets found at the housing project to any of the officer's weapons . . . . ." Crosby's article then quotes Austin as saying, "[T]he matter was fully investigated and presented to the grand jury, which took no official action."

It is hard to believe that Kennerly's rampage was actually presented to the grand jury as none of the three officers involved was called to testify. In fact, it is obvious that these unbelievable incidents of criminal conduct were known by State Attorney Austin and his office and completely covered up. This is Obstruction of Justice 101.

In addition, Austin is also wrong when he claimed there were no corroborating witnesses. Jim Lucas, the owner of Guys and Dolls, in a later 1979 FDLE investigative report ordered by Governor Bob Graham, revealed that he had gone to the Sheriff's Office and told them that Kennerly was known to him and had shot up his place of business and home.

In 1979, Lee Cody had occasion to interview the Lucas family. The family said that even though the shootings into their home and business were reported, their complaints were never fully investigated. Eventually one detective, Detective Lieutenant Joe Kicklighter, did appear in response to their complaints and advised the Lucas family that drug dealers had done the shooting into their business and home and they should be very careful. Other than that, there was no effort ever made interview witnesses. Nor did any police officer appear to attempt to gather ballistic evidence from either the victims' place of business or their home.

In 2008, Lee Cody learned that former Jacksonville police officer and witness Jack Jones was residing in North Carolina and still had the same .44 magnum in his possession that Kennerly had used. In conversations with Officer Jack Jones through the years, Jones revealed that at no time since the original incident has anyone from the Duval County Sheriff's Office or the Florida Fourth Judicial State Attorney's Office ever requested him to release that .44 magnum revolver for ballistic testing. During this time frame, Jack Jones revealed that neither he nor Danny Howard was ever subpoenaed to testify before a grand jury regarding Kennerly's terrorist rampage.

In light of information like this, how can one seriously believe Austin's claim in his January 6, 1975 letter to Governor Askew's Assistant General Counsel Donald Middlebrooks that he would "carry out" his responsibilities (i.e., prosecute anyone) in any dealings with Sheriff's Carson's department?

If State Attorney Austin was not deliberately making sure that his close personal friends and associates, particularly Sheriff Dale Carson and State Attorney William A. Hallowes III, would not fall in harm's way, some decisions he made certainly seemed to be fortunate for his friends. For example, in his January 1975 letter to Governor Askew's General Counsel Donald Middlebrooks Austin avowed his commitment to prosecute any criminal activity he had knowledge of. However, Austin requested on February 26, 1975, only one month later, that the entire War on Crime investigative file collected by the Wackenhut agency be shredded. Be mindful that this was an investigation Austin had nothing to do with and that those documents contained extremely damaging evidence against both Carson and Hallowes, and if for no other reason than Cody's previous communication to Austin in 1969, he had to have known that. Beyond all doubt, this destruction of collected state evidence is a blatant example of Austin's continued efforts to obstruct justice. This was more than just "misplacing" a letter or hiding a file under a mat. This was deliberate destruction of evidence. This file was massive--22 cubic feet in 14 boxes. Paul A. Rowell, attorney for the FDLE, forwarded Cody a record of Austin's destruct order. A copy of this destruct order is still in Cody's possession along with the original envelope and cover letter that accompanied it from FDLE General Counsel Paul A. Rowell.

Is it any wonder that Cody's last words in a follow-up letter to Governor Askew were, "We do not need further investigation, we need prosecution."

On the same day that Howard's deposition was delivered to Austin (3 April 1979), Cody and investigative reporter Al Parsons presented a copy of Officer Howard's deposition to the Jacksonville office of the FBI. As they had done in 1964, the FBI personnel in Jacksonville, FL chose once again to protect Sheriff Dale Carson from exposure or prosecution.

In 1998, in response to a Freedom of Information Act query, a document was forwarded to Cody that contained a partially redacted FBI complaint form, dated April 9, 1979, which addresses allegations that, Ron Kennerly, a former officer of the Jacksonville Sheriff's Office, shot up automobiles and other property on 11/04/74 but was never prosecuted for his actions, and therefore the victims did not receive due process of law. Also received in the FOIA submission package were the front sheet and the errata sheet from the sworn deposition of Florida Highway Patrolman Danny Howard, which had been transcribed on April 3, 1979. A stamp on the FBI complaint form is dated April 8, 1980 and indicates that on that date this case was closed and a box marked with an X states, "No further action being taken." There is no indication on any investigative form in the FOIA submission that eyewitness Florida Highway Patrol Officer Danny Howard, Officer Jack Jones, or the terrorist detective Ron Kennerly were ever interviewed or even contacted by the FBI.

It would have been impossible for the FBI to reach an investigative conclusion regarding the criminal conduct of Jacksonville Sheriff's officer Ron Kennerly without interviewing all three of these fact witnesses. The Jacksonville Office of the FBI, as they did in 1964, beyond all doubt, protected Sheriff Dale Carson and the office of

151

the Fourth Judicial State Attorney Ed Austin, et al., allowing those guilty public officials to escape detection and detention or to face the bar of justice in any way.

In addition, not only did the power brokers of Duval County politics and law enforcement agencies help the guilty escape prosecution, they used their position to punish the innocent. Here are two examples, both involving Ron Kennerly, the terrorist JSO officer who shot up Jacksonville.

Jack Jones, who had covered up Kennerly's shooting rampage and had supplied him with the .44 magnum revolver, was the first to suffer, even though he was Kennerly's best friend. Perhaps fearful that Jones would reveal his criminal conduct, Kennerly sought to discredit Jones by entrapment. In Kennerly's twisted mind, he thought that if Jones were branded as a thief, nothing Jones said about Kennerly would be taken seriously should Kennerly's actions become public knowledge. Kennerly worked as security officer for the apartment he lived in. He called Jones, who he knew was building a house in the country, and said, "Hey, a contractor friend gave me some lumber for a deer stand. It's stacked here on the apartment property. Bring your truck out here and we'll load it up."

Meanwhile, Kennerly alerted his superiors in the Sheriff's Office that Jones was intending to steal the lumber. Jones arrived in his pickup truck and he and Kennerly loaded the wood. They left together, but were soon stopped and arrested by JSO personnel charged with grand theft. Though ostensibly arrested, he was not charged, as he was working undercover. Kennerly's story was that Jones had asked him to help steal the lumber.

As already pointed out, there is no doubt that the Jacksonville Sheriff's Office knew of Kennerly's shooting rampage. They knew other things, too. Kennerly was known as Undersheriff D.K. Brown's boy. The new Jacksonville Undersheriff, along with Sheriff Carson, turned a blind eye to Kennerly's antics and past reputation.

Kennerly knew things too. Cody once saw Kennerly in a Jacksonville Bar on a Saturday night. Kennerly was drunk and running his mouth, but had no idea who Cody was. Kennerly bragged to the friends surrounding him, "They can't fuck with me. I know where all the guns and bodies are buried."

Coming from a compulsively violent man whose life was in a constant manic meltdown, a rogue cop who had recently raped his ex-wife with a Coke bottle, such statements must be taken seriously.

The second illustration of how the guilty were punished by these power brokers is even more amazing, and it also involved Kennerly.

JSO officer Donald Greene managed to get on Sheriff Carson's bad side. Likely, this was due to the fact that, like Jack Jones, he was working with a union-organizing movement in the JSO. Sheriff's Office administrators had warned both men that it was not in their best interest to continue these union-organizing efforts.

Though the Jacksonville Sheriff's Office knew about Kennerly's criminal activities, instead of prosecuting him, the Sheriff's Office used Kennerly's testimony to indict Greene for the alleged sale/delivery of a controlled substance—a twenty-dollar bag of marijuana. Greene was convicted and sentenced to five years in prison on the perjured testimony of Kennerly. In addition, Kennerly set up a sting through his ex-wife that resulted in the arrest of Barry Zisser, Greene's lawyer, also for drug charges. This was an obvious frame, yet it still affected Zisser's career and reputation negatively.

The District Court of Appeals eventually overturned Greene's conviction and Greene was exonerated, released from prison, and reinstated to his job by the Civil Service Board. Yet through his powerful judicial connections, Sheriff Carson was able to successfully appeal the board's decision and terminate Greene's employment and revoke Greene's police officer certification.

Kennerly's poorly conceived plan to eliminate both of the eyewitnesses to his criminal activity eventually backfired on him. First of all, Jones felt betrayed by Kennerly and quickly revealed to his legal counsel the details of Kennerly's shooting rampage. Jones' lawyer notified the State Attorney's Office, who notified the Florida Highway Patrol, and it is only reasonable to assume that Sheriff Carson was also notified. Howard did lose his employment with the Highway Patrol through termination. However, Kennerly was allowed to resign from the Sheriff's Office with a glowing letter of recommendation from Sheriff Dale Carson.

Cody interviewed Jerry H. McMillan, an executive with Crowley Maritime Corporation who revealed that he had hired Kennerly after he left the Sheriff's Office. "Seeking Better Employment" reared its ugly head again and Kennerly was made head of security for Crowley Maritime Corporation's San Juan, Puerto Rico facility. McMillan told Cody the primary reason he hired Kennerly was because of the glowing letter Sheriff Carson had written that had outlined what an outstanding officer Kennerly had been.

This conduct of the Jacksonville Office of the FBI and the Jacksonville Sheriff's Office must be categorized as criminal. Steve Croft, correspondent for the CBS news magazine *60 Minutes* describes the corruption in Duval County well. In her piece, "Shots in the Dark," Susan Armstrong, *Folio Weekly* reporter, quotes Croft as saying,

154

"Greene's case was a travesty, but came to typify the JSO. . . . The Sheriff's Office seemed above the law. There was no shortage of rumor and allegation involving serious misconduct . . . It was clear Ed Austin had no interest in prosecuting [Carson's JSO]."

To further exacerbate this horrible and incredible miscarriage of justice, on August 2, 1999, former Detective Sergeant Cody posted a certified letter to Lewis Freeh, Director of the FBI in Washington D.C., a letter that was received and totally ignored by FBI Director Freeh. In the letter, Cody reiterated his concerns and allegations that he could prove that the FBI had:

1. In 1964, had itself obstructed justice by its failure to investigate the criminal act of obstruction of justice reported to them by Jacksonville Sheriff's Office detectives, Sergeants Cody and Coleman and FBI Agent Robert McCarthy.
2. Received reports of documented Civil Rights Violations that were never investigated.
3. Covered up the criminal Civil Rights violations committed by Jacksonville Sherriff's Office, Certified Officer, Deputy Sheriff, Detective Ronald Kennerly.

If perhaps a copy of the *14th Denial* somehow finds its way into the hands of the current FBI Director, he will have the common decency and feel the obligations of his office and reply to this author.

Chapter Eighteen:
This Is Bob—Governor Bob Graham 1979-87

*The American people have been denied important
information for their own protection.*
—Bob Graham

In October of 1979, when Cody traveled to Tallahassee to secure a private investigative license, he was sitting in the capitol vestibule, when a gentleman approached him and introduced himself. The man said his name was Dave Columbo and that he worked for Governor Graham. Columbo was an aide to Richard Schoditsch, who was Assistant General Counsel to Governor Graham. He asked Cody where he was from. When Cody replied, "Jacksonville," the man nodded and said, "Oh, did you know that Ed Austin, Fourth Judicial Attorney from Jacksonville, had just been appointed a special prosecutor for the purpose of prosecuting Florida State Educational Commissioner Floyd T. Christian and others?"

Cody replied that he did not know that news.

Columbo continued. "Do you know Ed Austin?" he asked. And as if he assumed Cody did indeed know Austin, Columbo said, "What do you think of him?"

Cody replied, "Well, Mr. Columbo, I think that if anyone needs prosecuting, it's Ed Austin."

Mr. Columbo said, "Why in the world would you say that?"

"Well, primarily because I have personally investigated Mr. Austin's professional conduct and can prove that in many instances he has violated his oath of office by obstructing justice and I personally think that he should be languishing in a very secure prison."

Mr. Columbo almost fainted. "Oh, my God. Come with me."

He escorted Cody into an office and introduced him to Richard Schoditsch who identified himself as Assistant General Counsel to Governor Graham and who headed the Office of Executive Prosecution. Mr. Columbo related to Mr. Schoditsch what Cody had said about Ed Austin.

Mr. Schoditsch said, "Can you prove these allegations? If so, I'm anxious to hear what you know. Please have a seat and let's discuss what you know."

After Cody and Schoditsch conversed a while, Cody said, "Instead of talking to me in generalities here, if you really are interested in knowing about Ed Austin's criminality, I think it would be more appropriate to send your investigators to Jacksonville to counsel with me and other witnesses I will furnish and to view documented evidence that I will supply, and then let them return to Tallahassee with that witness list and documentation for your evaluation."

Things appeared to begin moving. On October 9, 1979, Richard Schoditsch forwarded a letter to Commissioner James W. York, Executive Director of Florida Department of Law Enforcement, and the letter's contents read in part, "I would appreciate your contacting Mr. Cody and evaluating whatever information he may furnish you. *And please advise me as to any recommendations you may have as to recommended action.*"

On October 11, FDLE inspector Arthur S. Avirom was dispatched to Jacksonville by the Governor's office. Upon arrival, he met with former Detective Sergeant Cody, former Detective Sergeant Claude West, and investigative reporter Alpheus Parsons. Inspector Avirom spent several days with them, hearing testimony, viewing documentation, and obtaining a witness list. He then returned to Tallahassee. Inspector Avirom called soon after his return and shared with Cody what the FDLE recommendations to the governor would be. Avirom gave these same recommendations to Chief Inspector Patrick J. Doyle. In a memorandum he says:

> I agree with Mr. Cody who stated in his letter to Governor Askew of 23 April 1976, "We do not need further investigations, we need prosecution," that it would serve no useful purpose to open an investigation by this agency. If the prosecutive route is followed either through a statewide Grand Jury or through an outside State Attorney the files previously compiled can be used. In addition, the witnesses not called during the previous Grand Juries could be examined.

Expecting this to happen, Cody was ecstatic at the news. However, his exultation was short-lived. On January 4, 1980, Cody received a letter from Schoditsch indicating that the governor's office had decided not to follow the FDLE's recommendation.

On February 4, 1980, Cody forwarded a letter contesting the decision and asking the governor's office to reevaluate their lack of action. On February 15, Cody received another letter from Schoditsch repeating their position—in essence; the governor's office would not follow the FDLE's decision. Unbelievably, in his last letter, Schoditsch recommended that if Cody was unhappy with

159

this decision, Cody could go directly to the current foreman of the Duval County grand jury—a jury guided and advised by Ed Austin, the man Cody accused of criminal obstruction of justice. Did Schoditsch think Austin would confess to the grand jury his criminality, advise them to indict him, and then turn himself in to the Warden of the State Penitentiary?

To Cody and his fellow patriots, it seemed that Austin too was beyond incrimination. This was another battle they apparently could not win, and they basically threw in the towel. The detectives concluded that it was more important to the governor to avoid embarrassment of having appointed a corrupt special prosecutor rather than to do the right thing—which would be to respect our nation's rule of law and expose and punish Austin and the other public officials whose names and criminal acts were furnished to the FDLE.

About 1982, a public statement was made by Federal prosecutor known as Robert "Mad Dog" Merkle. He said he was impaneling a grand jury in Tampa for the purpose of investigating public corruption in Florida. He said that if anyone had any information at all regarding corruption in Florida to contact his office. In response to this public announcement, even though still discouraged over Governor Graham's failure to fulfill his oath of office, Cody decided to try one more time.

Cody contacted "Mad Dog's' office and was subpoenaed to appear before the impaneled Federal Grand Jury in Tampa, Florida. Cody immediately responded and upon arrival at the Federal courthouse in Tampa, he was escorted to a room where an assistant U.S. Attorney interviewed him for several hours. During that interview, Cody delivered the same evidence that he had previously furnished the FDLE for Governor Graham. The assistant attorney seemed shocked at the revelations. He told Cody there was not time for Cody to appear that day before the grand jury, but he thanked Cody and said that Cody would again be subpoenaed to appear before the grand jury at the earliest possible date.

That never happened. Cody repeatedly tried in vain to contact Merkle's office by telephone and could never reach anyone to talk to.

About a week later, the news media learned that Cody had been subpoenaed and contacted Merkle's office about Cody's subpoena. They asked if this meant that Sheriff Dale Carson was once again under investigation. Merkle's office emphatically replied, *No, Sheriff Carson was not under investigation.*

After this setback, Cody and his patriot friends were absolutely convinced that because a large portion of the evidence submitted to Merkle's office clearly and beyond all doubt implicated the Jacksonville Office of the FBI in criminal conduct, the evidence was covered up again. As far as guarding society against crime and public corruption, Mad Dog Merkle's bark was much worse than his bite, and in the opinion C. Lee Cody, Merkle joined the already long list of obstructors of justice.

*   *   *

Years, passed. Then in 1996, an event occurred that gave new life to his decades long quest for justice. Though he still continued to write letters to U.S. Attorneys, there was a time when Cody more or less gave up his quest. He had been through four governors, a number of state and federal prosecutors, the FBI, many jobs, and after giving most of the best years of his life, had lost more personally than he cared to think about. All his work for all those years seemed to have been spent for nothing.

He also truly missed his job with the Sheriff's Office. He still remembered one day not long after his termination, when he had stopped at a traffic light and a patrol car stopped next to him. Cody was driving a garbage truck from the Jacksonville shipyard, the only place in town where could find employment.

"How do you like your new job, Lee?" one of the officers said.

"I'm getting along alright."

The light changed and they sped off. Cody was deeply hurt by their attitude. These were men he had once worked closely with.

For a while, Cody lived on a little houseboat on Jacksonville Beach. He did not take the local newspaper or watch television. A weary man now, he did not want any more controversy. When you live at a marina, you use the marina facilities. One morning, he had to walk past the bar to get to the showers. On his way back to his houseboat, he happened to see on the top of a tall bar table a newspaper article with a photo of a young black man kneeling by a gravestone in Jacksonville's Greenwood Cemetery. Cody saw in the article that the young man's name was Shelton Chapell. *My lord God*, Cody thought. *That must be Johnnie Mae's son.* Shelton had only been months old when his mother had been murdered.

Cody picked up the newspaper. The article was about a memorial service that would be held the next day at Mount Ararat Baptist Church. Cody felt an urge to go to the memorial service and reveal to the Chappell family how their mother's 14th Amendment Civil Rights had been criminally violated with impunity by Florida State attorneys, Florida governors, the FBI, and state and federal prosecutors.

Cody anguished over the decision as to whether he should go to the service. He had served in the Coast Guard during the Korean War on a cutter that had been re-outfitted in Baltimore with the latest antisubmarine equipment. After the refitting, his ship was assigned to patrol certain areas of the Caribbean, particularly around Cuba. During those many days at sea, the personnel aboard his ship were subjected to a constant barrage of antisubmarine warfare drills. This required that large numbers of depth charges be dropped. Cody's assignment during general quarters was in the aft end of the ship. In that era, the majority of the piping was insulated with asbestos. When the depth charges would detonate, the aft end of the ship would receive most of the effects of the exploding depth charges. These violent explosions would jar the dry asbestos that surrounded the piping loose and shower down upon anyone stationed in the aft steering room. For several year, this routine filled his lungs with asbestos, and sometime later he was diagnosed with asbestosis, resulting in his having only 47% lung capacity. In addition to his asbestosis, Cody had also suffered a serious injury to his right knee when he fell from a ladder while at sea during a heavy storm.

In short, Cody felt his mortality. He was not in the best of health and was approaching his 70th birthday, and knowing his own determined nature, he knew that if he began helping the Chappell family, he would be subjecting himself once again to a great deal of mental, physical, and emotional stress and trauma.

He thought about it, his conscience took over, and he decided to go. He knew that if he did not, Shelton and the other members of the Chappell family would never be able to discover the truth. If for no other reason, there were only two fact witnesses alive who could testify against their mother's murderers and against the high-powered public officials who had violated their mother's 14th Amendment Civil Rights.

The two fact witnesses were former Detective Sergeants Cannie Lee Cody, Jr. and Donald Ray Coleman, Sr.

After the memorial service, he asked Shelton to sit down with him in the church lobby. He told Shelton the reason he had come. Cody said, "I know you're searching for the truth about your mama, but you'll never know unless I tell you. You do not know who to talk to or what to say. The men who murdered your mother are certainly not going to divulge any information to you, nor will the public officials who violated your mother's guaranteed 14th Amendment Civil Rights."

Shelton's eyes filled up with tears. "Will you help us?" he said.

"Yeah, I'll help you. Call me."

The first time they talked on the phone, Shelton said, "Do you mind if I record this?"

"Not at all," Cody replied. Cody is not sure if Shelton actually recorded him or not. Cody recognized that Shelton was a decent and honorable young man, but he fully realized that he was unsophisticated in knowing how to work with law enforcement, media, records systems, or public officials. Lee Cody took that weight on his shoulders and made the calls, wrote the letters for Shelton that he needed, and made the media contacts for him with people who could help spread the story regarding how his mother's Civil Rights had been violated.

Cody began to collect every bit of evidence he could place his hands on in state and federal archives— evidence that he hoped would help the Chappell family.

Cody realized that some documents that might especially help the Chappell family's and his renewed search for justice would be any FDLE files or reports that Inspector Arthur Avirom had generated and submitted to Governor Graham in 1979-80—if any existed. Cody contacted John Kimner, Regional Legal Advisor at the FDLE office in Jacksonville. Cody explained as clearly as possible, when the reports he wanted could have been generated and what the reports—according to what Inspector Avirom had previously told him—should contain. John Kimner agreed to help find the reports if possible. Cody left his phone number, but never heard from Kimner. After a few days, Cody returned to the FDLE Jacksonville office and when he requested to speak to Kimner, the office personnel handed Cody a note from Mr. Kimner. The handwritten note said:

Mr. Cody: Tried calling you for the past few days, but couldn't get you at home. I heard back from Tallahassee. After a complete search, they can find no documents that relate to your request. Sorry we could not provide what you are seeking. Feel free to call me if you have any questions.

Not satisfied with Kimner's hand-written note, Cody contacted Kimner via telephone and asked that he be given a face-to-face meeting so he could be sure that Mr. Kimner understood the report he was seeking. Kimner agreed and the two met. On June 22, 1998, Mr. Cody received a typed letter from Mr. Kimner, which basically said:

As previously discussed, I have forwarded your most recent public record request to our Office of General Counsel in Tallahassee. They have searched our archived files in an attempt to locate the items you have requested. *Again, I have been advised that a diligent search of our records has disclosed no such*

165

correspondence still existing in the FDLE files. As such, I am unable to provide you with any records which are responsive to this request.

Still not satisfied with the FDLE explanation, in the company of Claude West, Cody proceeded to the State Archives in R.A. Gray building in Tallahassee. After their own *diligent search* of former Governor Graham's archival depository, the following documents were retrieved.

1) A memo (discussed in the previous chapter) from Arthur S. Avirom to Patrick J. Doyle, dated November 13, 1979. The memo read:

I agree with Mr. Cody who stated in his letter to Governor Askew of 23 April 1976, 'We do not need further investigations, we need prosecution,' that it would serve no useful purpose to open an investigation by this agency. If the prosecutive [sic.] route is followed either through a statewide Grand Jury or through an outside State Attorney the files previously compiled can be used. In addition the witnesses not called during the previous Grand Juries could be examined."

2) Accompanying Inspector Avirom's report was a letter from Patrick J. Doyle, Chief Inspector, FDLE—Inspector Avirom's immediate superior. The attached letter, addressed to Richard E. Schoditsch, reads as follows:

In response to your letter of 9 October 1979 to Commissioner York, we have provided you with an investigative report dated 12 November 1979, and two memorandums dated 6 & 13 November 1979. *The memorandum of 13 November 1979 concurs with my thoughts on this action.* As we have previously discussed, this information and other volumes of evidence are in custody of Mr. Cody.

Upon Cody and Wests' return to Jacksonville, Cody notified FDLE Attorney Kemner that he had obtained copies of the reports that he had requested. Kemner replied, "My God, where did you find them?" Cody told him.

On August 17, 1998, Cody received another letter from Kemner that said:

Dear Mr. Cody:

Enclosed herewith please find a copy of the investigative report which was the subject of your July 17, 1998 Public Records Request. I apologize for the delay; however, it took some time for our Tallahassee staff to locate this report in the Executive Investigations archives. The costs associated with the processing of this request have been waived. . . [Cody thought it generous of them to waive the expenses!]

3) While searching Bob Graham's archival depository in Tallahassee, Lee Cody and Claude West not only found Avirom's documents, but also found a handwritten note from Richard Schoditsch to Lamar Matthews, General Counsel to Governor Graham. This note was forwarded to Lamar Matthews after Cody's final letter to Richard E. Schoditsch, dated February 18, 1980, requesting assistance and asking the governor's office to reconsider their decision to not follow the FDLE's recommendations. The note read:

Lamar: Should I even respond? Anything said now would be a rehash of my letter of January 4 to him.

Dick

Lamar's reply read:

> Dick: I would him write a brief two or three sentence note saying he should do what you told him in your Jan. 4 letter and enclose a copy. Unanswered letters sometimes give cause for yet another complaint.
>
> Thanks,
>
> > Lamar.

This note sickened Cody and has had a traumatizing effect upon all those who have read it and had sought the assistance of Governor Bob Graham. For the governor's General Counsel Lamar Matthews to trivialize a fervent and justified plea for assistance and justice from the governor has to be considered a shining example of the turpitude and disregard for citizens that existed in the elected and appointed officials of Bob Graham's administration.

All copies of these numbered documents with archival stamps, series 884, the series assigned to Governor's Graham's administration, are in Cody's possession.

After two decades, one would think the oft-reported obstruction of justice would somehow come to an end.

Chapter Nineteen:
Jeb Bush's Dog & Pony Show

Politics is the art of postponing decisions
until they are no longer relevant.
--Henri Queuill

According to the NNDB website,
(http://www.nndb.com/people/646/ 000022580/) in
August 1994, a voter asked Jeb Bush what his
administration would do to help the black community.
His response (rather, two words of it) became an
instant classic:

"We have elected people year after year that say, 'I'm
going to do this for you,' " Bush replied. "Now it's time
to strive for a society where there is equality of
opportunity, not equality of results. . . . So I'm going to
answer your question by saying, 'Probably
nothing.' . . .

In this quest for justice, Governor Bush's phrase
"Probably nothing" rings loud and prophetically. The big
difference between Florida governors is usually focused on
whether the governor is a Democrat or Republican, but
when it came down to the Chappell case and politics in
Jacksonville, there is really very little difference. Both
parties have proven to be equally apathetic and ineffective.

Jeb Bush was the 43rd Governor of Florida (1999-
2007) and the fourth governor to encounter Lee Cody's
quest for justice—justice for Johnnie Mae Chappell, a
black American mother of ten and her family and for

himself and the other detectives who were victimized by the corrupt powers they opposed. For Chappell and for the detectives, Bush did virtually nothing. According to the statutes of Florida law and the Florida Constitution, "The Governor has the constitutional responsibility to take care that the laws be faithfully executed."

Cody says that he would like to make this statement for the record: He is of the opinion that Governor Jeb Bush had no intention of securing justice for the Chappell family.

Yet Cody, perhaps out of habit, wrote the new governor and once again presented his case. Once again, Cody was ignored. Cody wrote more letters—letters that were also ignored. Not one to be easily ignored, Cody enlisted the help of Florida Senator Anthony C. "Tony" Hill, Sr. Senator Hill wrote Governor Bush an eloquent and forceful letter dated November 24, 2004:

Dear Governor Bush:

Please be advised the family of Mrs. Jonnie Mae Chappell, who was murdered in Jacksonville in 1963 [1964] requested that State Attorney Harry Shorstein re-open her case and they have received a denial of that request.

I asked Mr. Shorstein for a detailed explanation of his denial, but his verbal explanation, as he was unwilling to submit a written one, did not address the question of why three men who were indicted by a grand jury were not tried for Mrs. Chappell's murder.

This letter is to request that you appoint an independent prosecutor to review Mrs. Jonnie Mae Chappell's murder, the previous investigation of the murdered, the grand jury indictments of Wayne Chessman, Elmer Kato and Eugene Davis in her murder and all other pertinent

170

matters related to her murder. The excuses given about the time frame that has lapsed and the rights of those accused of murdering Mrs. Chappell should not outweigh justice being rendered to Mrs. Chappell and her family. We all know if timeframes or the rights of those accused of such a heinous crime were legitimate excuses, cases like the 1963 Birmingham, Alabama Church bombing would not have been re-opened.

The Chappell family should have the right to see to it that the three additional men indicted in the murder of their mother—one was tried—are prosecuted to the full extent of the law, that their mother received the same treatment as every other citizen murdered and suspects are known, regardless of the final outcome.

If you are not personally familiar with [the] case and need more information to support that Mrs. Chappell's murder was not properly handled, written and or through live testimony, I can arrange for you to hear and or review the material. The documentation is too voluminous to include with this letter and or to expect you to personally review alone.

An independent prosecutor is needed to not only review all of the information, but to make sure that proper procedures are then followed.

Governor Bush, you can end this continuing injustice by appointing an independent prosecutor . . . .

The good senator's letter forced Governor Bush to take some sort of action, which Cody's letters had failed to do. Bush ordered the FDLE to investigate the Chappell homicide. After Cody learned of that directive, the former detective complained bitterly to the governor that he apparently had no understanding of the matters under consideration. The Chappell homicide had been investigated

171

and solved, resulting in four first-degree grand jury indictments. No further investigation of that crime was warranted or necessary. The time and expense would be a waste of personnel and resources. The matter that needs deciding is a legal matter, not an investigative matter—the only question needed answering was this: Can the state of Florida today prosecute Mrs. Chappell's three murderers? Can Chessman, Kato, and Davis—who had been released from their grand jury pre-meditated first degree murder indictments via an irrefutable act of malfeasance perpetrated by State Attorney William A. Hallowes, III—be held accountable?

Cody even went further and wrote a letter to FDLE Director Guy Tunnell explaining that there was no legal reason at all to involve his agency. Cody asked Director Tunnell to contact Governor Bush and ask the governor to release his agency from involvement in this matter. This letter too was unanswered and the FDLE retained their assignment. Cody persisted. His continual complaints resulted in Governor Bush dispatching Wendy Berger, Assistant General Counsel to Governor Bush to interview Cody and discuss the matter of FDLE involvement. After a lengthy conversation with Berger and Cody's presentation of a myriad of documents, Ms. Berger agreed with Cody's contention that this was a matter that should be decided by a legal decision—that there was no need for investigation, that they were, as Cody has said in his letter to Commissioner Tunnell, "jousting with windmills."

When Governor Bush continued to assign FDLE personnel, Cody contacted Ms. Berger and asked her why Governor Bush was so insistent that the FDLE be involved in the Chappell matter.

Berger replied, "The Governor just wants to make sure and investigate--"

"Investigate what?" Cody interrupted. "No investigative agency can decide if the three illegally released men can be prosecuted today. It's a legal matter."

"Now, Lee, I know you're passionate about this, but let the governor do what he wants to do."

"What the governor's doing is nothing but a dog and pony show."

Cody's conversations and contact with the Bush administration ceased. The FDLE agents stumbled and bumbled around Duval County for weeks. Cody thought how uncomfortable it must have been for those agents to ask questions that had already been answered decades ago and would have had no bearing at all on the matter at hand. Then the true mission of the FDLE agents became apparent. After reviewing the FDLE Investigative Summary related to the agents' work, it became apparent to Detectives Cody and Coleman that the real reason Governor Bush had insisted on FDLE involvement was to have his agents search every nook and cranny of Duval county for any witness or scrap of a document that would in any way refute Cody's charges of corruption and cover-up that followed the Chappell homicide. Cody feels Governor Bush resented Cody's goading pressure to do his job—a job he had avoided to that point.

To illustrate how far off track the agents were in their assignment, Elmer Kato and Wayne M. Chessman were interviewed by the FDLE during their visit to Jacksonville. According to the FDLE reports, "Kato was adamant in his request for immunity and stated that if he was given immunity he would divulge accurate information regarding the entire incident from start to finish."

However, neither Special Prosecutor Cervone nor any other FDLE investigator made Kato an offer of immunity, or asked him anything further on what he had to share and why it would be valuable, and Kato never told.

Chessman was also questioned and denied many of his earlier statements and much of what Cody had affirmed, though Chessman strangely admitted being present when Mrs. Chappell was shot.

Prior to the FDLE interview, in 2002, Elmer Kato approached Cody and Coleman in the Federal Courthouse in Jacksonville during a status hearing concerning the Chappell family's Civil Rights lawsuit filed against Carson and the Consolidated City of Jacksonville. Cody asked him directly how he, Chessman, and Davis managed to convince the state attorneys to *nolle pros* their first-degree grand jury murder indictments.

Kato answered, "We tried to get to the judge, but couldn't. We offered the State Attorney a bribe to cut us loose and he accepted." Kato then added, "When this is all over, you and Coleman contact me. I'll tell you how much it cost us, who delivered the money—I'll just tell you all about it."

Cody never met with Kato for that conversation, but he has a good idea that Kato would have revealed even more information and details. The FDLE also knew because Cody had related details of Kato's revelations long before the FDLE questioned Kato.

For the FDLE to have ignored Kato's offer has to be considered an incompetent decision or a deliberate desire to cover up the truth. Beyond all reasonable doubt, if in fact the office of State Attorney Hallowes accepted a bribe—as Kato claimed—to *nol-pros* the grand jury first degree murder indictments of Kato, Chessman, and Davis, it would dissipate to dust all the continued legal barriers that have been placed in the path of re-prosecution of these confessed killers by State Attorney Harry L. Shorstein and

Governor Bush's handpicked Special Prosecutor State Attorney William P. Cervone, especially the speedy trial barrier. If these defendants were re-indicted and they submitted a motion claiming a speedy-trial defense, any judge or panel of judges, in the opinion of C. Lee Cody and other professionally trained legal minds, would deny that motion. They would deny that motion for the simple reason that the release from custody of Mrs. Chappell's killers was the direct result of a criminal act by the state prosecutor and if granted *justice would be denied*.

As we near the end of this section on Governor Bush, it is only fair to examine the contents of the letter by Governor Bush's special prosecutor, William P. Cervone, dated May 5, 2006 and examine Cervone's statements and legal opinions, which again deny justice and allow the murderers of Johnnie Mae Chappell to remain at large and untried in the United States of America. Cody and a multitude of highly trained legal minds disagree with Cervone's expressed legal opinions for these reasons:

1. Its redundant and ludicrous to investigate a murder solved over four decades ago. Since there were arrests and grand jury indictments of the confessed killers, what is there to investigate? The only reason to reopen the case would be if new evidence was found and new witnesses came forward and in this case, that did not happen and could not happen. Why didn't Cervone recognize these facts and advise the governor to withdraw the FDLE? That inability to recognize these facts might well have been because of the rural nature of the Eighth Judicial Circuit of Florida, from whence State Attorney Cervone emanated. Cody thinks it would be fair to say that State Attorney Cervone would be better suited in deciding cases of cattle rustling and horse thievery than cases that concern major Civil Rights violations, decisions that

affect not only the state of Florida, but also our entire nation.

2. State Attorney Cervone stated that he had reviewed the voluminous investigative file prepared by the FDLE, prepared Nov. 30, 2005. Cody finds that disturbing because there is not one word in that summary that would help prosecute the illegally released murderers of Johnnie Mae Chappell. Furthermore, not one member of the FDLE could offer him any factual testimony that would in any way enhance his ability to prosecute those murderers. The fact is, the only two humans alive on planet Earth today who could offer Attorney Cervone any factual testimony surrounding the Chappell debacle or testify before a grand jury in an effort to re-prosecute her killers are former Detective Sergeants C. Lee Cody, Jr., Donald R. Coleman, Sr. and the Duval County court reporters. Surely, State Attorney Cervone possessed enough legal acumen to recognize this fact. Cervone only allotted fact witness Cody forty-five minutes of time, and allotted no time to interview fact witness Donald R. Coleman. Yet, Cervone claims in his written words to have continually counseled for many hours with FDLE personnel who could offer him not one word in the way of factual testimony to aid in his prosecutorial mission.

3. Attorney Cervone made every attempt to minimize the criminal conduct of the murderers of Johnnie Mae Chappell. For instance, in his letter to Governor Bush dated May 5, 2006, Cervone says, "Rich's conviction itself seems to have relied almost exclusively on his confession to shooting *at* the victim with the claimed intent of frightening her, rather than killing her." Cervone's entry here is absolutely contrary to the *corpus delecti* of the Chappell homicide, one of the many documents Cody provided Cervone. The court-reported confessions of shooter J.W. Rich, Wayne Chessman, and

Elmer Kato contain these words: "Let's go get a nigger." After that statement was made, the four men drove directly to the northwest quadrant of Duval County and deliberately and with malicious intent, shot Johnnie Mae Chappell to death. This sounds a little more serious than Cervone's statement that they were *trying to scare her*.

4. State Attorney Cervone opines that the conviction of Rich for the lesser-included offense of manslaughter was legally and factually permissible. This entry is interesting for no other reason than the fact that State Attorney Cervone knew from evidence and statements presented to him by fact-witness Lee Cody that the conviction of shooter J.W. Rich for the lesser included offense of manslaughter was the direct result of the criminal acts of malfeasance, misfeasance, and nonfeasance on the part of State Attorney William A. Hallowes, III. It is fair to ask, "Why would State Attorney Cervone, being aware of these crucial facts, not address them?"

5. Another statement of Cervone's must be labeled as incredulous. He says that given the lack of any remaining evidence against the defendants beyond their *mere presence* at the scene of Johnnie Mae Chappell's murder, he was of the opinion that it would be difficult to convict them of the first-degree grand jury murder indictments. Let's examine this. These defendants armed themselves, drove into the teeth of an ongoing race riot in downtown Jacksonville, agreed to "go get a nigger" and accompanied shooter Rich, watched him shoot and kill Johnnie Mae Chappell, helped conceal the murder weapon, and themselves concealed the crime for months. Their conduct and involvement before and after the fact, as outlined in their court-reported confessions, beyond all doubt was more insidious and serious than a matter of *mere presence*.

6.   In his letter to Governor Bush, Attorney Cervone embraces the speedy trial barrier, already addressed in earlier sections. Cervone ends his letter with this statement: "I am convinced that the FDLE has left no stone unturned and that everything that could be done has been done."

In response to that assertion, Cody would like to make this observation: There were no stones for the FDLE to turn over in the first place. Cody also feels that Mr. Cervone's comments were precipitated from ignorance, legal incompetence or malice aforethought. But regardless of why the state attorney took this position, Attorney Cervone has joined the long list of public officials who have obstructed justice in the quest to bring the illegally released, grand-jury indicted murderers of Johnnie Mae Chappell—Eugene Davis, Wayne Chessman, and Elmer Kato—before the bar of justice.

7. On March 26, 2006, Cody met with Attorney Cervone and provided him with a legal brief furnished to Cody by Lee Martin, Lead Counsel, Civil Rights Division for the State of Mississippi. Cody had discussed the Chappell case previously with State Attorney Martin and had discussed the viability of today prosecuting the illegally released murderers of Johnnie Mae Chappell. Prosecutor Martin digested the information quickly and was of the opinion that the only question that could be raised by any of the defendants would be as to whether or not they were denied *due process*. In his opinion, a speedy trial barrier presented by the defendants could not stand. He went on to say that in order for a defendant to be successful in claiming they had been denied due process, the defendant would have to prove that in this case the state delayed their re-indictment and prosecution to gain a tactical advantage. As he understood the facts of the Chappell case, the defendants would be unsuccessful in proving

this. State Attorney Martin also pointed out that in their successful delayed prosecutions in Mississippi Civil Rights cases; his office had utilized Florida state law to bolster their prosecutorial ability. Two of the Florida cases addressed the act of *nolle pros*--Gibson verses State 26 Florida 109 7 So. 376 as well as Smith verses State 185 Fla. 835 188 So. 208 1989. The Florida Supreme Court held that nolle pros did not hinder the re-indictment of a defendant on the same charge. Cody informed Cervone that Martin advised that he would be more than glad to assist Florida prosecutors in any way that he could. Mr. Martin furnished Cody his office number 601-35904261, which Cody in turn provided to Cervone. Later Cody inquired as to whether Mr. Cervone had contacted Mr. Martin. He was told that no request for assistance had been received. Cody has often wondered why Attorney Cervone, who had limited Civil Rights litigation experience, would not accept the offer of assistance from Assistant Attorney General Jim Martin, the preeminent Civil Rights litigator in the nation.

8. On May 5, 2006, Attorney Cervone met with Cody, Chappell family members and their attorney, Robert Spohrer, in Cervone's Gainesville office. As the meeting was about to conclude, Cody said to Attorney Cervone, "There is one more small matter I'd like to bring to your attention. I have just finished reading the letter you have written to Governor Bush and in that letter, you indicated that have relied heavily on the FDLE research in making your decision. This is not understandable to me. In the letter you stated that you had made one final attempt to make sure that nothing had been overlooked and every stone overturned. So let me now direct you to page twenty of the recently compiled FDLE summary. There you will find an interview with one of the illegally released grand jury indicted murderers, Elmer Kato. Mr. Kato offered to exchange information for immunity—accurate infor-

179

mation on the entire incident from start to finish. FDLE inspectors O'Connell and Westveer who conducted the interview never asked Kato what information he would like to divulge. What he wanted to divulge was that he and Chessman and Davis were released because they had bribed the State Attorney's Office." Cody continued. "I previously communicated this compelling information to both you and to inspectors O'Connell and Westveer." Cody then asked, "Don't you realize that if Kato could be allowed to relate these facts to a grand jury, then there is a high probability that the speedy trial and the other barriers you and State Attorney Shorstein have so fondly embraced could be defeated?"

State Attorney Cervone replied, "The Governor didn't ask me to investigate that."

Cody replied, "I don't believe you could have the audacity to make a statement like that." Cody rose to leave the room, but was persuaded to remain by Attorney Spohrer, but he had nothing else to say.

To this day, the evidence clearly shows that special prosecutor Cervone did not intend to prosecute the three illegally released killers of Johnnie Mae Chappell and feels that his prosecutorial conduct was preprogrammed from the office of Florida Governor Jeb Bush.

On May 16, 2006, Lee Cody posted one final letter to Governor Jeb Bush stating again that the flawed legal conclusions of State Attorneys William Cervone and Harry Shorstein should not stand. The last paragraph in that letter contains these words, "Governor I now reluctantly conclude my 42 year battle to secure the rights of a humble black American mother, a battle which it seems at this juncture, I have lost. But in losing, I have learned and history has taught me two things. First, being a patriot is not an easy task. Second, corrupt politicians are hard wired, simply put they are a class of individuals who cannot feel remorse, violate the law with impunity, and have an absolute distain for our nations laws and its honor." This posting was ignored by Governor Bush.

The conduct of former Governor Jeb Bush and his circus ringmaster, William P. Cervone, can only be described one way—as a pathetic insult to a decades long constitutional injury suffered by a citizen of our nation, Johnnie Mae Chappell, a law-abiding black mother of ten children, who as John Brown, lies moldering in her grave while her grand jury indicted and illegally released murderers walk free in our land today.

Yet, to be fair, the Bush administration's conduct was no more disgusting and obstructive than the public officials who proceeded or followed them.

Chapter Twenty:
Johnnie Mae's Legacy

There is a strange charm in the hope of a
good legacy that wonderfully reduces
the sorrow people otherwise may feel
for the death of their relatives and friends

--Miguel de Cervantes Saavedra

In October 2008, former Detective Sergeants Lee Cody and Donald Coleman in their continued quest for justice in the Chappell family requested and were granted a meeting with newly elected Florida Fourth Judicial Circuit State Attorney Angela Corey, and once again shared their story and their belief that Governor Jeb Bush had intentionally neglected his responsibilities. They also stated that they believe the men who had committed these crimes against Johnnie Mae Chappell and obstructed justice could still be prosecuted. They once again shared their extensive mountain of evidence, thinking that perhaps this time Florida might have a State Attorney who had the will to prosecute the killers.

State Attorney Angela Corey received the information, thanked them, and said she would be in touch soon. Having not heard from State Attorney Corey for weeks, Cody, feeling that Attorney Corey could not fully comprehend the importance and quantity of the evidence she had been provided, followed up their first meeting by mailing her a detailed outline of events surrounding the Chappell homicide and cover-up.

Again, Cody never heard from her. Cody said he should have expected this response for when she was a candidate for State Attorney; he had approached her, shared the general, horrific details of the Chappell homicide cover-up and asked if she would consider reviewing the evidence he had collected. She said she would be happy to look at whatever evidence Cody could present.

However, she also said, "Oh my God, I hope none of this involves Ed. He was so good to me." Cody's heart sank for he knew she had been one of Ed Austin's assistants when Austin was State Attorney, but Cody had faith in Corey's integrity and was certain that that this past connection would not stand in the way of justice. After all, at this point he was *not* asking State Attorney Corey to prosecute former State Attorney Ed Austin, though he surely deserved prosecution, but to prosecute the killers of Johnnie Mae Chappell.

Attorney Corey's ensuing silence deeply concerned Cody. Attorney Corey needed to meet with Cody and Coleman face to face so they could help her understand the evidence Cody had provided and place the details and the massive amount of evidence he had collected in proper context. Without meeting with the detectives, it would be impossible for State Attorney Corey to understand what had happened and to appreciate the voluminous complexity of the documents and evidence he had collected through the years.

Did her silence indicate that she, like the others in public office who had heard Johnnie Mae's story, had no intention of making a legitimate effort to punish those who had violated Mrs. Chappell's constitutional rights? State Attorney Corey is the only one who can answer this question. State Attorney Corey never replied and she will never know how she devastated those who trusted her, especially Shelton Chappell.

According to Shelton, when he met with State Attorney Corey, she hugged him and assured him that everything would be all right and that *justice would prevail*.

It did not.

———

The following document was delivered to State Attorney Angela Corey in a last ditch attempt to legally reason with her. As of the date of publication of this book, State Attorney Corey has chosen not to respond.

Forward:

Both State Attorney Harry L. Shorstein and State Attorney William P. Cervone recently decided that prosecution today of the three individuals named Wayne M. Chessman, Elmer L. Kato and James A. Davis who were complicit conspirators in the death of a black American woman named Johnnie Mae Chappell was not possible.

Both State Attorney's Shorstein and Cervone cited three legal barriers that would preclude in their opinion prosecution today in this case. Barriers which are enumerated as follows:

1. Speedy Trial Guidelines
2. The Proportionality Doctrine.
3. Statute of Limitations.

Each of these barriers will receive legal examination in the text of this document to determine if either one of the three can maintain legal status in this case, or should ever have?

Before the legal objection to barriers 1, 2 and 3 are transcribed herein. Facts, which will assist State Attorney Corey's understanding of the enormity of the prosecutorial criminal conduct prevalent in the Chappell homicide, will be transcribed herein. A copy of a letter posted by fact witness C. Lee Cody, to then State Attorney Harry L. Shorstein that clearly explains this stated criminal conduct is attached. It is imperative that the legal explanations contained within the letter to State Attorney Shorstein be examined by State Attorney Corey to assist her understanding of this matter. Obviously, any effort by State Attorney Corey to re-indict and prosecute the individuals responsible for the death of Johnnie Mae Chappell will rely to a great degree on her exposure to the facts. All the needed facts that are contained in the letter to State Attorney Shorstein were submitted to State Attorney Cervone prior to his final legal opinion forwarded to then Governor Jeb Bush. Sadly, State Attorney Cervone as well as State Attorney Shorstein chose to disregard this crucial evidence.

OBSERVATIONS:

1. On The night of March 23, 1964, when Mrs. Chappell's death occurred, two separate criminal offenses were committed. Defendant J. W. Rich shot and killed Mrs. Chappell. Defendants Wayne M. Chessman, Elmer L. Kato and James A. Davis were complicit conspirators before and after Mrs. Chappell's death. The "Corpus Delecti" of the Chappell homicide firmly establishes these facts. A document titled "Corpus Delecti" is attached. Further, it had to be abundantly clear to a State Prosecutor with forty plus years of prosecutorial experience that two distinctly different crimes had occurred which necessitated two different evidence presentations to a jury. Clearly making the fact that two separate indictments were required not one. To bolster the two-indictment requirement on November 5, 1964, Circuit Court Judge John McNatt recognized that rudimentary necessity. On

186

that date he issued an order of severance (attached) To Witt: Ordered and adjudged that a severance be, and the same is hereby granted in this case as between the defendants J.W. Rich on one hand and the defendants Wayne M. Chessman, Elmer L. Kato and James A. Davis on the other hand, so as to permit and allow the state of Florida to proceed to trial against the defendant J. W. Rich, separate and apart from the trial against the defendants Wayne M. Chessman, Elmer L. Kato and James A. Davis (severance order attached).

2.   Both State Attorney's Shorstein and Cervone continued, verbally and in writing claimed that they have repeatedly solicited the assistance and guidance of the Florida Department of Law Enforcement in matters surrounding the homicide of Johnnie Mae Chappell. For the record there is not now nor has there been in the recent past any present employee of the Florida Department of Law Enforcement that could furnish State Attorney's Shorstein and Cervone on iota of factual evidence or testimony that would have impacted one way or the other their ability to legally decide if illegally released grand jury indicted conspirators Wayne M. Chessman, Elmer M. Kato and James A. Davis could today face prosecution for their criminal conduct in 1964.   Their continual references for their need to confer with members of the Florida Department of Law Enforcement can be considered nothing more than political subterfuge designed to convince the legally untrained and politically naïve that they were engaged in a relentless ongoing quest for justice for Johnnie Mae Chappell. Bottom line, the Florida Department of Law Enforcement was improperly inserted in this quest for justice by Florida Governor Jeb Bush. To solidify this opinion be reminded that the Johnnie Mae Chappell homicide was cleared by the arrest of her four assailants and no further investigation of that homicide in 2006, 2007 or 2008 or for that fact forever was needed or warranted. Also Governor Bush clearly understood this. Because this fact witness writer

187

explained this fact to his Assistant General Counsel Wendy Burger in a face-to-face meeting in Jacksonville, Florida.

3. It must be noted that both State Attorney's Shorstein and Cervone were furnished undeniable documented evidence that in 1979 the Florida Department of Law Enforcement Inspector Arthur Avirom was dispatched to Jacksonville Florida by Florida Governor Robert Graham to receive evidence from former Duval County Sheriff Department Detective Sergeants C. Lee Cody, Claude R. West and Investigative Reporter Alpheous Parsons. The volumes of evidence received by Inspector Avirom included the criminal obstruction of justice prevalent in the investigation of the homicide of Johnnie Mae Chappell, as well as the criminal conduct of Prosecutor William A. Hallowes, III. It is most compelling to note that neither State Attorney Shorstein nor Cervone ever mentioned their knowledge of this 1979 Florida Department of Law Enforcement's involvement. It is fair to ask and would be compelling to know why State Attorney's Shorstein and Cervone never mentioned that Inspector Avirom at a date much closer to the event, recommended to Governor Robert Graham that a special prosecutor or a state wide Grand Jury be given the evidence that had been furnished for prosecutorial consideration. That factual question has an easy answer. Inspector Avirom's recommendations were absolutely in direct conflict with State Attorney Shorstein, State Attorney Cervone and the Florida Department of Law Enforcement recently cited legal opinions regarding the prosecution of Mrs. Chappell's killers. Obviously, if those facts were made public they would devastate the validity of State Attorneys Shorstein and Cervone's publicly stated legal assumptions. And brand Governor Graham just another obstructer of justice.

BARRIERS:

1. Speedy Trial Guidelines.

Question: Does the speedy trial barrier in this case cited by both State Attorney Shorstein and Cervone have any legal validity?

Answer: Absolutely not. The most compelling fact to support legal opposition to cited speedy trial barrier assumptions in this case must be the existence of documented evidence that proves beyond all doubt that the State Prosecutor William A. Hallowes, III criminal act of releasing grand jury indicted complicit conspiratorial killers Wayne M. Chessman, Elmer M. Kato and James A. Davis via (nolle pros) was not because of the officially cited (insufficient evidence) court progress docket entry but was a premeditated act of malfeasance designed to obstruct justice. Just this documented act of malfeasance alone by the State Prosecutor clearly should negate any legitimate speedy trial barrier. This malfeasance meets every legal requirement necessary to be an Exception Circumstance delineated in the Florida statute addressing speedy trial considerations. For either State Attorney Shorstein or Cervone not to have considered the compelling undeniable readily available documented factual evidence which had been furnished to them both must be considered a deliberate act of nonfeasance. Both Sate Attorney's Shorstein and Cervone are declaring in essence that defendants Chessman, Kato and Davis as well as any other defendant taken into custody by the state o Florida on a felony charge prior to the speedy trial guidelines implementation on November 1, 1971, and had not been afforded a trial within this specified one hundred and seventy-five days contained within those rules could make the assertion today that their Constitutional guarantee of a speedy trial had been violated has to be considered ASTONISHING. Both State Attorneys Shorstein and Cervone knew or certainly should have known prior to the 1971 speedy trial guideline insertions that all prior speedy trial contentions were adjudicated on a case-to-case basis.

189

It is abundantly clear that this seriously flawed reasoning would in turn allow not only Chessman, Kato and Davis but every felon convicted by the state of Florida prior to November 1, 1971 and not tried prior to the one hundred and seventy-five day guideline requirement implemented years later an avenue to petition the courts for a new trial in an attempt to have their convictions overturned. In addition, State Attorney Shorstein and Cervone knew or certainly should have know that absent specific legislative intent all legislative statutory insertions are by long standing custom, practice and tradition considered pro-active not retro-active. The 1971 Speedy Trial Rules contained no such specific retroactive guidelines.

It is also important to note that content of the lengthy conversations this writer held with Jim Martin the lead civil rights prosecutor from the office of Mississippi Attorney General Jim Hood. Assistant Attorney General Martin revealed that the speedy trial barrier had been repeatedly raised by the defense councils in successful civil rights prosecutions that he had conducted, and each and every time the speedy trial barrier had been defeated. The Mississippi State Prosecutor opined after learning the facts of the Chappell homicide that in his opinion the only argument any of the defendants involved in the homicide of Johnnie Mae Chappell could offer up would be that Due Process had been denied them. If a Due Process argument became an issue in the Chappell case it would fail miserably. Primarily, because the onus would be on the defendants to show that the state deliberately delayed prosecution to gain a tactical advantage. In this case, that argument would have unobtainable success. Also of vast importance is the fact that Mississippi Assistant Attorney General Martin forwarded to this writer two standing Florida Supreme Court decisions titled as follows: Smith vs. The State of Florida 26 FL, 109 7 S. 376 and Gibson vs. The State of Florida 109 7 S. 376. In both cases, the Supreme Court found that a "nolle pros" of charges does not release a defendant from the original jeopardy. This writer furnished State Attorney Cervone this compelling legalese prior to his decision letter to Governor Jeb Bush, which he ignored. He also ignored a standing invitation for legal assistance from Assistant Attorney General Jim Martin, who's direct phone number he was furnished.

2. The Proportionality Doctrine:

Question: Would the fact that shooter J.W. Rich was convicted of the lesser included offence of Manslaughter preclude the State of Florida from prosecuting today conspirators Chessman, Kato and Davis for the crime of Premeditated First Degree Murder as charged by the Grand Jury?

Answer: Absolutely Not.

Shooter J.W. Rich was not convicted of the lesser included crime of Manslaughter because he was not guilty as charged by the Grand Jury, but because State Prosecutor William A. Hallowes, III, working in undeniable concert with Defense Counsel committed a multitude of criminal acts which resulted in shooter Rich's Manslaughter conviction. To Wit: Misintroduction of ballistic evidence, failure to require testimony of crucial witnesses, etc. Further, it is extremely troubling, that State Attorney Shorstein would raise the "Portionality Doctrine" considering these facts. In the early 1990's two black males Tyrone Sutton and Clifton Clark committed several violent armed robberies in Duval County. During the commission of robbing a restaurant on the Arlington Expressway's "Cisco's" Tyrone Sutton shot and killed a member of the Cisco staff. The office of State Attorney Shorstein prosecuted both of these criminals. It is compelling to note that Tyron Sutton (shooter) received a total sentence of fifty-nine years' incarceration while complicate conspirator Clifton Clark was tried and received a life sentence. Considering these verifiable court records for State Attorney Shorstein to render an opinion that the "Proportionality Doctrine" would in part bar prosecution of Johnnie Mae Chappell's indicted killers are absolutely contrary and in total conflict with the official prosecutorial

191

record of his own office. All of the foregoing facts were given in detail to State Attorney Cervone, which he obviously intentionally again disregarded while making his final prosecutorial decisions regarding the murder's of Johnnie Mae Chappell.

3. Statute of Limitations:

Question: Does Statute of Limitation have any legal standing regarding the Chappell homicide?

Answer: Absolutely Not.

If shooter J. W. Rich had been legally tried and legally convicted of a lesser-included offense the Statute of Limitation argument would be very weighty. However, there is no reasonable legal way that the illegally tried shooter J. W. Rich's conviction of the lesser-included offense of Manslaughter could in anyway deny state prosecution of conspirators Chessman, Kato and Davis for the crime of Premeditated First Degree Murder for which they were indicted by a dually paneled Grand Jury.

Finally, I think it appropriate that to include in this document the opinions of Attorney Robert Spohrer regarding re-indictment of Mrs. Chappell's violators posted to Special Prosecutor William P. Cervone on March 2, 2006.

Mr. Cervone, we respectfully suggest that there are compelling equitable arguments for convening a Grand Jury to consider re-indictment of the Chappell perpetrators. Those arguments include the widespread racial tensions in north Florida in 1964 and later years, the now openly acknowledged corruption which existed in the Sheriff's Office at the time, the unexplained disappearance of the court files, the murder weapon and confessions, and finally, the inexplicable decision of the state to nolle pros three men indicted for the first degree murder with no explanation to the victim's family nor document explaining the rationale for this decision. The states of Mississippi and Alabama have brought to

192

the Bar of Justice perpetrators of hate crimes from the sixties; the State of Florida should do no less. Although the Chappell murder may present close questions of law and fact, we firmly believe that these questions should be resolved in a courtroom, by a judge and jury, rather than peremptorily rejected by the state. The will of the 1964 Grand Jury in indicting four men for murder has never been carried out, and we do not believe it to be a violation of any prosecutorial ethics to permit the court system to conclude its work in this matter.

Submitted in the respect for the rule of law and justice for all.

NOTE: Fact witness C. Lee Cody, Jr. is solely responsible for the content of this document.

Signed: C. Lee Cody, Jr.

CC: Shelton Chappell
       Keith Beauchamp
       U.S. Attorney Middle District of Florida
       The Honorable Robert E. O'Neill

———

Since his first meeting with Shelton, Cody has spent hundreds of hours trying to help the world learn the story of Johnnie Mae Chappell.

Cody knew they had to get Shelton and his mother's story to the media. At the beginning of Cody's efforts, it was difficult to find anyone interested. Cody eventually reached Adam Smith of the *St. Petersburg Times*. They were not interested at first, but Cody persisted.

Finally, Smith called Cody and said, "I've talked to my editor and he said we could do the story of Johnnie Mae Chappell."

Smith drove up and spent the day with Cody and the paper soon printed the first story.

The Southern Poverty Law Center picked up Johnnie Mae's story from the Internet and began inquiring about the case themselves. The SPLC contacted Cody and Shelton Chappell and good things began to happen and Johnnie Mae Chappell's story, the one that had vanished from the Duval County Sheriff's Office records so long ago, that story began to be told.

First Allison Orr, the producer of *Dateline*, also responded to Cody's query. *Dateline* staff came to Jacksonville, interviewed Cody and did a wonderful piece. Then for some reason, Orr called Cody and said they decided to not run it. Something happened, and then a few months later, *Dateline* contacted Cody and said that now they decided to run it. They had lost the original production and would have to return to Jacksonville and redo it.

Then, the Dateline program was followed by a production on *Court TV*.

Oprah Winfrey also decided to tell the Chappell story and included it as part of the Martin Luther King Memorial she ran in January of 2008.

Not long after the program ran on *Oprah*, a New York filmmaker named Keith Beauchamp contacted Cody. He said he had been retained by the History Channel to do a documentary about Civil Rights issues, and of all the stories he knew about, he had chosen the Johnnie Mae Chappell story to be the one most newsworthy and compelling. He asked for Cody's assistance. Cody again agreed and informed Beauchamp that he possessed volumes of evidence that would document and prove the flagrant violations of her Civil Rights. The film was made and entitled, *Wanted Justice: Johnnie Mae Chappell.* The film is a wonderful tribute to Johnnie Mae's Memory and the History Channel production was aired on Feb. 26, 2009.

Her legacy lives on. Johnnie Mae Chappell Parkway in Jacksonville was named in her honor. The highway extends along U.S. Highway 1 North, beginning at the spot where she was murdered. A memorial sign was placed along that highway, as well as a plaque honoring her at the Southern Poverty Law Center in Montgomery, Alabama.

After the filming in Jacksonville was over, Keith Beauchamp said to Cody. "I just can't believe that you have the corruption documented like you do. You need to write a book."

And with that conversation, the idea for this book was born. Maybe this book will make a difference. Maybe Johnnie Mae Chappell's story will be told at last. Moreover, just maybe fact witnesses Detectives Sergeants C. Lee Cody, Donald R. Coleman and Court Reporters Eddie and Leo Powell will be allowed to present to a duly impaneled Grand Jury the 14th Amendment Constitutional violations contained in this publication. Violations suffered by Johnnie Mae Chappell and others. A presentation unjustly _denied_ for over four decades.

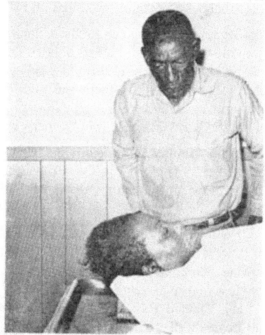

NEGRO STUDENTS TO STRIKE BACK

Willie Chappell laments death of wife, Mrs. Johnnie Mae Chappell, who was killed during white mob's bloody rampage

A VIOLENT END: This 1964 photo, from[11] JET magazine, is the only image Willie Chappell had of his wife, Johnnie Mae

Fig. 1. Johnnie Mae Chappell

Fig. 2. Left to right: Kato, Chessman, and Rich before Judge Jessie
Leigh. C. Lee Cody stands to the right.

Fig. 3. Detectives Claude West, C. Lee Cody, and Donald Coleman

Fig. 4. C. Lee Cody and Donald Coleman at the Southern
Poverty Law Center, which was rededicated to Johnnie Mae
Chappell.

Fig. 5. U.S. 1 where Mrs. Chappell was killed was
designated the Johnnie Mae Chappell Parkway

Fig. 6. C. Lee Cody, Shelton Chappell, and Donald Coleman

CPSIA information can be obtained
at www.ICGtesting.com
Printed in the USA
LVHW092145110819
627284LV00003B/19/P

9 780557 599677